KT-166-509

CLASSIC ADVENTURES

This book belongs to

Name . . . .

Date . . . .

Robin Hood

Robin Hood

Retold by
Charles Wilson

The Classic Adventures Series

First published by George G. Harrap & Co
This facsimile edition
© Fabbri Publishing Ltd 1991
Printed and bound in Spain by Printer
Industria Gráfica, Barcelona

ISBN 1-85587-329-X

Contents

CHAPTER   PAGE

I. ROBIN IS OUTLAWED 9

II. THE MEETING OF ROBIN HOOD AND LITTLE JOHN 16

III. THE WEDDING OF ALLAN-A-DALE . . . 24

IV. ROBIN AND THE CURTAL FRIAR . . . 32

V. THE SHERIFF DINES WITH ROBIN HOOD . . 40

VI. HOW THE BISHOP PAID THE RECKONING . . 50

VII. CONCERNING SIR RICHARD OF THE LEA . . 57

VIII. REYNOLD GREENLEAFE 65

IX. ROBIN QUARRELS WITH LITTLE JOHN AND IS CAPTURED BY THE SHERIFF . . . 74

X. THE SAVING OF WILL STUTELY . . . 86

XI. SIR RICHARD REPAYS HIS DEBT . . . 94

XII. HOW THREE BOLD ARCHERS FOUGHT THREE BRAVE FORESTERS 104

XIII. ROBIN IS BEATEN BY A BEGGAR AND RESCUES THE WIDOW'S THREE SONS . . . 111

XIV. MAID MARIAN 120

CHAPTER   PAGE

XV. The King's Archery Contest at Finsbury
        Field   129

XVI. King Richard Visits Sherwood Forest   .   137

XVII. The Marriage and Death of Robin Hood   149

ROBIN HOOD: his Merry Exploits

Chapter I

Robin is Outlawed

BRIGHTLY shone the sun, and a gentle breeze played upon the glorious green of the trees, now in their beautiful hue of spring.

And because it was spring, and the day was bright, young Robin tramped blithely on his way. In his hand he gripped his trusty staff, and over his shoulder carried his bow of yew, whilst at his side swung a quiver full of arrows. He was a stalwart young man and clad from top to toe in cloth of Lincoln green.

The road down which he strode so gaily was the one between Gamwell Hall and proud Nottingham town. Lightly he stepped, with his shoulders well back and whistling a merry air, for the Sheriff had proclaimed an archery contest, and offered a golden arrow as the prize to the best marksman. This was the long-awaited morning, and he was off to the meeting, care-free and happy, yet so eager for the contest that ever and anon his fingers strayed and lingered lovingly upon his bowstring.

His way led through Sherwood Forest, and he had not gone far along the woodland road, under the overhanging oaks, when a harsh laugh broke in upon his song. Looking aside, Robin saw coming out of a bypath a party of King's foresters, and with them their chief, a cross-grained, ill-humoured fellow, by name Gruff—and never was man more aptly called than he. Small reason had the young man to like this surly official, for Robin's father had once been head forester, and this man, by trickery and low cunning, had taken the position from him, and caused him to be cast into Nottingham Jail, where, languishing for the greenwoods and the open sky, he slowly died.

Singing no longer, but holding his head high, Robin ignored the rude laughter and would have passed on, but the keeper blocked his way and scoffed at the lad, calling to his men to admire the dainty child's bow and arrows. They also, no whit behind their master, directed all manner of coarse jeers toward him. Still disdaining a reply, Robin evaded his tormentors and went his way, pursued by vile abuse and gibes.

He had proceeded about fifty paces when abuse changed to action, and an arrow whizzed by, within an inch of Robin's ear. Turning immediately, he saw Gruff fixing a second arrow, and his pent-up passion could be restrained no longer. "Thou murderer," he cried, "wouldst kill the son as thou didst the father?"

The forester, with black rage in his heart, loosed the second shaft at Robin's breast, but the young man jumped lightly aside and the arrow did but graze his arm.

To fix and shoot was but the work of an instant to Robin, and righteous anger steadied his aim, for the head forester, turning to flee, pitched headlong with the arrow through his heart.

With angry shouts, the foresters crowded round their chief, but finding he was past all aid, left two of their number to guard the body, whilst they set off in hot pursuit of Robin.

Robin was fleet of foot, and, knowing his life was at stake, he ran with such speed that in a few minutes he out-distanced his pursuers, and was able to gain, unperceived, a secret glade in the very heart of the forest. For a while he lay perfectly still, listening for the crackle of twigs, which might warn him of his enemies' approach.

With his courage restored, he thought of a way by which he might even yet attend the meeting and win the golden arrow. So, smiling the while, he tore his cloak in ribbons and made the other parts of his apparel look as shabby as he could; and after no long delay a dirty and seemingly destitute vagrant with tattered garments limped out of Robin's retreat and slowly wended his way toward Nottingham.

As he approached the town, Robin dropped his limp, and, pulling the hood of his cloak well over his face, he mingled freely with the crowd. He listened with befitting wonder to the rumour of the death of Gruff, the King's forester, for already each man was whispering the news to his neighbour.

In a right happy mood was the holiday crowd, and laughter and shouting told of the bouts of wrestling and quarter-staff which filled in the time before the shooting contest, which was eagerly awaited by all. So the time sped till three o'clock struck and the Sheriff was due to appear. A great flourish of trumpets and the Sheriff, accompanied by his daughter and many attendants, entered the field. They took their appointed seats, upon a raised platform, and the lady signalled that the shooting was to begin.

Tall men and short men, lean men and fat men, grey-beards and striplings lined up at the butts, and amongst them the beggar. How the crowd laughed when he threw off his cloak and revealed his tattered garments. But not in the least daunted, he smiled back at the people and patiently awaited his turn, when every arrow he loosed came to rest in the centre of the target. Rapidly the marksmen thinned out, and the crowd, seeing the beggar could shoot a likely shaft, and liking his smiling if dirty face, now cheered every arrow he loosed.

Soon there remained but four men. Two were King's foresters, one a short, fat stranger, and the fourth was the beggar. These now prepared for the final round and the target was placed so far away that it could scarce be seen.

A hum of approval greeted the shots of the foresters, for each had hit the target, though only in the outer ring. Next came the turn of the short stranger, and a great shout went up, for his arrow was found quivering within an inch of the centre of the target. "Now, friend beggar i' th' hood," shouted a wag from the crowd, "an thou beatest that, the arrow is thine !"

Most carefully fitting the shaft, Robin took aim and shot with all his craft.

True flew the arrow through the air; it smote hard and true, right in the centre of the bull's-eye, and a delighted shout proclaimed the beggar's victory.

"By my troth," laughed the fat stranger rue-fully, "there goes the Sheriff's arrow. 'Twas a rare shaft, young man, and here's Will Stutely's hand on't."

By this time the crowd had surged round the victor and shoulder high they bore him to the presence of the Sheriff. With due formality this worthy proclaimed him the "best archer and dirtiest rogue" in all Nottingham. Then the proud maiden, his daughter, who had never before touched a beggar, pinned the golden arrow to his cloak, whilst the crowd roared with glee: "A Hood! A Hood!"

Leaving the crowded scene of the contest, Robin made his way to the town and soon found himself in the great market-place. Hearing a trumpet, and seeing people flocking to a space before the old Moot Hall, he arrived just as an officer began to read the following proclamation by the Sheriff of Nottinghamshire:

"One, Robin, nephew of Squire Gamwell of Gamwell Hall, having murdered the King's head forester, is hereby declared an outlaw. Furthermore, a reward of One Hundred Pounds will be paid for the capture of the said Robin alive or dead."

The trumpeters sounded a final flourish, the officer and his company departed, and laughter and merriment were the order of the day.

But the beggar did not stay long in the town with his golden arrow; once outside the gates, he made straight for the forest and so to his secret glade.

Chapter II

The Meeting of Robin Hood and Little John

A MILE out of Nottingham Robin overtook a short, sturdy figure, whom he quickly recognized to be none other than his unsuccessful rival of the afternoon's sport.

"Give thee greeting," said Robin, smiling. "Whither art thou bound?"

"Hello! my ragged friend," replied the sturdy one in a deep voice, "whither goest thou?"

"No home have I save the forest," said Robin sadly; "no bed save the moss under the greenwood tree."

"How art thou called, beggar?" inquired Will.

"My name is Robin——" But thinking of the price set upon his head, he said no more.

"Methinketh Robin is a good name," and, glancing at the hood, Will continued: "Our friends at the contest called thee 'A Hood,' so I'll call thee Robin Hood."

Robin at once appropriated the title and

exclaimed : "Truly hast thou guessed, good friend ; henceforth Robin Hood is my name."

"Mine thou already knowest," quoth Will. "And if Will Stutely had not a liking for the King's deer and a somewhat natural desire to keep his ears, he would not now be sought by the fat Bishop of Hereford. Why, his lordship seems to be as fond of ears as I of venison, and thou— of head foresters," he added, with a wink.

"I perceive thou knowest me," said Robin, and, glad of a listener, he repeated the whole story.

Honest Will was much moved, and assured Robin of his sympathy. "Thou didst well," he added simply. "I be but a plain man, but I like thy fellowship. If thou'lt have me, I'll stay with thee in the forest and be thy man."

"With all my heart," eagerly cried Robin, and the two wended their way together to the retreat in the glade.

Time passed ; young men of spirit heard of the two outlaws, and further attracted by the free life of the greenwood, they joined them, so that in due course Robin was the leader of some fifty stalwart and merry men, whose delight was in the chase and all other manly sport, and whose favourite dish was venison.

One bright morning in summer up rose Robin from his grassy bed, and slinging his quiver across his shoulders, and with bow in hand, he took the road to Nottingham town, hoping for an adventure.

His way led through the forest, and across his path ran a swiftly flowing brook, spanned by a single plank. As Robin drew nearer the narrow bridge he saw a huge, ungainly giant, about seven feet high, approaching on the other side. For a staff he carried a young oak sapling. Robin hurried, that he might cross first, but the stranger also quickened his pace, so that they met in the middle of the plank.

"Give way, fellow!" roared the giant in a voice like thunder.

"Give way thyself," retorted Robin hotly, "or I'll pitch thee in the stream, big as thou art."

"Ho! Ho!" laughed the big man in his beard. "Thou'lt pitch me in the stream? Ho! Ho! Ho! Ho!" and in his merriment he almost toppled over into the water.

"Just wait a second, thou huge oaf, and I'll tan thy hide for thee," snapped Robin. Quickly he cut himself a staff and lightly sprang upon the narrow bridge. "Wilt give way first?" he cried to the laughing giant, and raising his staff, brought it down upon the fellow's crown with a crack that ended all laughter. "Not I," came the answer in a roar of pain, and with great force the oak sapling struck Robin's ribs. Crack again fell Robin's weapon and the giant grunted with the force of the blow. So the fight went on. Hard blows were exchanged, and a stifled exclamation from one or the other, a grunt or a sharp cry of pain only sent the staves swinging swifter than before.

Full half an hour they fought thus, and never before were jackets so well beaten. Their breath came in quick, short gasps, but so equal were they in skill that neither had given or taken a foot-length of the plank past the centre. The giant, who dearly loved a tussle of this kind, still smiled happily, and Robin smiled also, for a fight was meat and drink to him.

The giant's smile, however, hid some cunning, and, pretending to aim a buffet at his adversary's ribs, he suddenly changed the direction of his attack and dealt Robin one hard blow upon his head that sent him staggering and almost caused him to lose his precarious foothold.

Recovering instantly, and feeling he could never tire the giant out, the outlaw started to belabour him right merrily. First his head, then his ribs, now his head again, and then his ribs once more, till the poor man thought that the sky must be raining cudgels upon him. Suddenly a tremendous blow caught him unaware on the shoulder and down he dropped on one knee. Another whack across his ribs that would have killed a lesser man sent him swaying, and as Robin held his staff in mid-air, prepared to deal the final blow that was to send his opponent into the stream, the giant righted himself, and, standing up, dealt Robin such a crack across his head that he sent that poor youth struggling into mid-stream.

"Ho! my fine friend," panted the giant as he rubbed his aching ribs, "where art thou now?"

"Swimming right merrily," answered Robin untruthfully, for his head hummed mightily from the force of that last blow.

Sore and bedraggled, Robin pulled himself out of the water and up the bank, and still the giant stood laughing at the plight of his unfortunate adversary.

Shaking from himself as much water as possible, Robin blew a long blast upon the horn that he always carried as leader of the band, and as he paused the giant asked if he might be allowed to complete the process by beating the water from his clothes. Robin would have replied with further blows, but Will Stutely and a dozen more of the band rushed out from the trees and laid firm and not

THE TUSSLE BETWEEN ROBIN HOOD AND LITTLE JOHN

gentle hands upon the giant, and on perceiving
that their beloved master had lost the fight,
they proceeded to take their own revenge.
Holding him so tight that he could not move
a limb, the party carried him to the edge of
the water and with a "One, two, three," and
a mighty swing, they hove him right into
mid-stream, where he disappeared from view.
Quickly Robin jumped upon the bridge and
in mockingly smooth tones inquired : "Prithee,
my fine comrade, and where art *thou* now?"

A vigorous splashing was the only answer,
and in a trice the giant set foot upon ground
and had Will Stutely bowled over before that
astonished youth could lift his arm. Three
others were treated in the same manner, and
then the remaining archers flung themselves
on him in a body and dragged him down. Yet
still he breathed defiance, and offered to fight
them all, three at a time.

"No more!" cried Robin. "Thou art the
likeliest man that ever I have met, and we'll
fight no more." After further words of good
will the giant stumbled to his feet, and, assured
of their friendship, shook hands all round.
Having thoroughly regained his good humour
by now, he inquired the whereabouts of one
Robin Hood, who lived in these parts, and he

added: "I am a forester of Mansfield and desire to join his band."

A great roar of laughter followed his request, as Robin replied: "And so indeed thou shalt, for I am Robin, and these men here are of my band."

A look of delighted surprise lit up the face of the stranger. "Master," said he humbly, after a long pause, "master, would I had given thee way first." And then more cheerfully: "But indeed I will the more willingly serve thee, for surely thou strikest so hard, I could love thee for it."

"But hold!" cried Robin. "Thou hast not yet told us thy name."

"I had forgotten," said he. "I am called John of Mansfield."

"Join our band and welcome, John. As thou art such a stripling, it were well to call thee 'Little John,'" cried Robin, and every man stepped up in his turn and smote the giant's broad back as a sign of good-fellowship.

He had not been a member of the party very long before the band grew larger and it became necessary to appoint a lieutenant to aid Robin; Little John was voted by one and all to that position.

Chapter III

The Wedding of Allan-a-Dale

"COME along," called Robin to his tall lieutenant one day. "Let us seek an adventure to give an appetite for our midday meal."

"Yea, master," readily assented Little John. "And may Our Lady send us a bishop."

'Twas a cloudless morning, and as it was too hot to walk very far they sat down by the roadside to wait.

Presently they spied a young man coming along the road and singing at the top of his voice a merry love-song.

"I' faith," whispered the giant, "methinketh yonder stripling is in love!"

"What a man thou art for noticing things," chuckled Robin. "Surely, wedding-bells will soon be ringing for him."

With amusement in their eyes, they watched the young man till a bend of the road hid him from further view; then with a light laugh Robin jumped quickly to his feet, saying:

ROBIN HOOD FIRST SEES ALLAN-A-DALE

"Our laugh has given us an appetite for our dinner!"

Next morning they took up the same position as on the day before, and whilst waiting for company fell to talking of the scarlet stripling of yesterday. Presently round the bend in the

road there came limping a poor, bedraggled
wretch, with clothes in shreds, and as he came
nearer they saw with surprise that the colour
had been bright red.

"'Tis our friend of yesterday," whispered
Little John excitedly. "He's been roughly
handled too, poor fellow."

Robin scarcely heard the words, for, leaping
to his feet, he reached the miserable man in a
few strides. "Didst not pass this way yesterday?" inquired Robin gently. "And wast thou
not then carolling right merrily?"

"Too true," groaned the other, and made as if
to pass on.

"Nay, friend!" declared Robin, his heart
stirred with pity at sight of such misery.
"What is thy trouble? If it be in my power
to help, right willingly will I, or my name is not
Robin Hood!"

"Nor mine Little John," came in husky tones
from the tender-hearted giant.

Recognizing these names, the young man
plucked up courage and told his sorrowful tale.
His name was Allan-a-Dale, he told them, and he
dearly loved a maid and she him, and they were
to have been married that very morning, but a
certain rich Norman lord had cast his eyes
upon the maid, and because her parents were

avaricious, she was to be forced to become the Norman's bride. She had been taken to his great castle, and they were to be married by the Bishop of Hereford.

Said Robin with an angry light in his eyes: "And how camest thou in such plight?"

Said poor Allan: "Surely, I did go to the castle and demand my love, but the Baron scoffed at me from the battlements and sent his men to beat me." And then, with righteous pride shining in his eyes, he added: "I broke the heads of two, three more I flung into the moat, and one is mourned as dead. What more could man do?" he asked simply. "The rest beat me sorely and with many gibes drove me away."

"Now we know thee for a true man," answered Robin, "and willingly will we help thee."

After further questioning it was found that the church was but five miles away and the wedding fixed for three of that very afternoon.

"Smile, Allan lad. See, the sun hath not yet reached its zenith, yet before it sets thy lady shall be restored to thee, and as she thinketh to be married by my lord Bishop, 'twere a shame to disappoint her," continued Robin cheerfully.

Placing his horn to his lips, the outlaw chief blew one loud blast that brought many fellows dressed in green from all directions, with their quivers slung over shoulders and their bows in hand.

"Who's for a wedding, lads?" questioned Robin, smiling. "All of us!" responded the men as one voice, and even poor Allan-a-Dale was seen to smile at their enthusiasm.

"Where's Will?" called Robin. "Here, master," replied stout Will Stutely, stepping forward. "Take thou our friend Allan and clothe him in the finest scarlet cloth from our store, and bring him outside the church of St Mary over the hill by three o'clock, for the happy man is to be married," ordered the leader, and added quickly: "See to it thou art in good time, for we must not keep the Bishop of Hereford waiting."

Will straightway bore the astonished Allan to their secret abode, where he fitted him with such finery as became a bridegroom.

Half-past two saw some strange companies on their way to the little church. First arrived the Norman lord, an old man, and with him the fat and pompous Bishop, followed by their company of retainers. Hardly had they settled in their places when in strolled a tall fellow, a minstrel by appearance.

"Whom have we here?" rapped out the Bishop in angry tones. Smiled Robin: "I am a harper brave and bold, and the best in the north countrie!"

"Welcome, welcome," replied the Bishop in conciliatory tones. "Right fond of the harp am I. Come take thy stand near me!" Robin obeyed with alacrity, and just then there appeared at the church door the bride, supported on either side by her heartless parents.

The old Baron hobbled forward to greet her, but the maiden stopped and shuddered as she turned her head away with great despair in her misty blue eyes. The groom halted too, and looked round with astonishment when a loud blast rang through the church and far into the fields beyond.

Just as the echoes died away, and the people were getting alarmed and restless, a party of fifty archers, all bravely dressed, strode into the church. Little John, as leader, conducted them right up to the very steps of the altar, where his first act was to lift the old Baron with one hand and pitch him amongst his terror-stricken men. The bowmen then broke ranks and through them stepped a now transformed Allan. Splendidly dressed, and with a happy smile, he took the vacant place by the bewildered bride. Casting aside his harp, Robin turned to the maid and with a smile questioned her: "Fair maiden, since it is the custom to marry but one husband, and here we see two bridegrooms—pray choose the one, that the ceremony may proceed." But by this time the maid had recognized her own dear love, and was sobbing happily on Allan's breast.

"She hath well chosen," declared Robin. "A young man and love is ay to be preferred to an old man with riches. Hasten with the marriage service, reverend Bishop!"

"I know thee—thief and robber!" screamed the enraged Bishop. "I'll not marry them either. For the law of the land thus demands —'Three times shall the banns be called from the altar.' Thou hast overstepped thy mark this time." After saying which he shut his book with a snap and sat upon it.

"Come hither, Little John. What manner of bishop wilt thou make, I wonder?" asked Robin, whilst the bowmen stripped off the robes of the Bishop, who was purple with rage, dismay, and indignation, and put them on the laughing giant. Leaving the old Churchman still sitting upon his precious book, they turned to contemplate the new dignitary, whose garments hardly reached to his knees. With mock dignity Little John proclaimed the banns. Addressing the gallery, again he called them, and to the people gathered below, yet again. Full six times he called the banns, and for the seventh he stood specially in front of the outraged Baron and shamefaced Bishop, who were protected on three sides by bodies of stalwart men in green, and again he called the banns.

Never before were banns called in such a voice and with such fervour. The Bishop, perceiving that he was outwitted, and very cleverly too, called out: "Give me back my gown and I'll marry them, aye, and bless them too."

"Good," replied Robin. "Thou shalt have double fees for this, I warrant thee."

"Who giveth this maid?" came in a subdued tone from the true bishop, who had by now again donned his robes. "I do!" responded Robin heartily. "And any man who shall attempt to take her from Allan-a-Dale shall reckon with Robin Hood of Sherwood and Barnesdale."

After this wise was Allan-a-Dale married to his lady fair.

Chapter IV

Robin and the Curtal Friar

DURING the happy summer months that followed Robin and his merry men often held trials of skill amongst themselves, sometimes in Sherwood and sometimes in more northern Barnesdale.

After one of these contests in Barnesdale Robin was walking with several of his best archers, and together they discussed the recent match, when a herd of deer was seen to be passing in the distance, and Will Stutely, without much ado, fixed his shaft, and a noble buck fell to the earth, pierced by his arrow.

"Well shot!" exclaimed Robin. "Canst equal that, friend Much?"

"Nay, master, for the deer are now fled and the distance is great; but here's for a try," replied Much the Miller. Fitting the action to the words, he loosed his shaft and brought down a young doe that was slightly behind the herd. Robin gave a joyous shout of approval and looked inquiringly at Little John. "I'll do my best!"

smiled that giant, and standing erect as a young tree, he took careful aim and shot with all his strength. The arrow whizzed through the air and was lost to sight, when a noble hart, the leader of the herd, sprang high in the air, and then fell heavily to earth.

"A finer shot I never saw," quoth Robin proudly, when Will interrupted with : "Say not so, master, for I know a sturdy friar who could beat either shot, aye, and thine own too, master," for he was a little jealous of the praise bestowed upon his comrade.

"Sayest thou so?" asked Robin, slightly jealous of the skill of an utter stranger. "Bring hither the man and I'll prove thy words untrue."

"'Tis the curtal friar of Fountains Abbey, and a stronger bow and stouter man at all manly games there never was."

"He will have to thank thee for a drubbing then, for to-morrow I'll find this man and he will find his master," replied the leader.

Early next morning Robin arose and set off, well pleased at the thought of meeting such a worthy foe. As he approached the riverside he saw, strolling along the bank, a huge and burly monk, dressed in gown of brown cloth and with a girdle about his middle, but, unlike any other monk, he wore a knight's cap of steel upon his shaven crown. Also, there hung a sword by his side, and a large bag and bottle balanced it on the other side. Robin soon discovered the contents of these latter, for, sitting down, the knightly monk drew a good-sized pasty from the bag, and, first taking a long pull at the bottle, proceeded to dispatch the pie.

"Ha! Ha!" laughed Robin softly. "Methinks this is the man I seek, and venison pasty happens to be just the dish I love most. I'll seek a quarrel with him and test his prowess." Stepping quietly, he suddenly presented himself before the friar, who looked him calmly up and down and then went on with his meal. When next he glanced up he caught the glint of the sun on the arrow pointed straight at his heart. Not wishing to be done to death whilst life was so sweet to him, he laid down the pasty and listened whilst Robin spoke. "Good Friar, yonder water looketh wet and I have ever been cautioned against wetting my feet. I pray thee, therefore, to carry me over to the opposite bank."

Nothing ruffled at this impudent demand, he replied: "Methinks thou art a ready fellow, but because it is my duty to render aid to the weak and helpless, I'll carry thee across."

Robin clambered upon the broad back offered

ROBIN HOOD AND THE CURTAL FRIAR

him and without further speech he entered the
water and was landed safely on the opposite
bank. With a merry laugh the outlaw leapt
lightly down, but paused in an instant, for
the friar's sword was pricking at his tunic.
"Stranger," remarked the monk, with a merry
twinkle in his eyes, "sorry I am to trouble thee,
but my dinner awaits on the other side, and
as one good turn deserves another, surely thou
wilt now carry me back?"

There being no escape, Robin had perforce to
hoist the heavy monk upon his slim shoulders
and bear him across, not, however, without
much stumbling and splashing, for the man was
extremely weighty. Moreover, his sword had
constantly pricked Robin on to quicker effort,
and it was no wonder that he landed panting
and breathless. By a subtle movement, however, Robin possessed himself of his adversary's
sword and addressed himself thus to that worthy:
"Grieved am I that I cannot stay to dinner with
thee, for time presses and I am in great haste.
Prepare, therefore, and carry me over the water,"
and added as he saw the friar hesitate and
prepare to continue his dinner: "I'll give thee
such a drubbing if thou dost not obey that thou
shalt be sore for many a day!"

Without a word, and with almost suspicious

meekness, the friar bent and took the other upon his back and made his way to mid-stream, where, with a forward heave, he pitched Robin over into the deepest part of the water.

"Now choose. Sink or swim, my fine fellow," and turning his back upon the struggling man he waded to shore and sat down to his pie.

Hardly had he done so when the outlaw, knee-deep in water, clambered up the bank. Seizing his bow, he loosed a shaft that must readily have found the friar's heart had not that man quickly moved aside so that it sped harmlessly by. Quickly jumping up, and anxious only to defend himself, all Robin's arrows glanced off his buckler, and when not one remained Robin drew sword, and hand to hand they fought a long and equal fight. Up and down the bank, sometimes ankle-deep in mud, round and round they went, and still the decisive blow had not yet been struck. For nearly an hour they fought thus, equally matched and each on the look-out for a point of vantage. By a clever feint the friar struck Robin a heavy blow on his head that almost drove the steel cap through the skull. The outlaw dropped on to one knee, dazed and panting, and feeling he had lost the fight he craved one last boon.

"What is it?" shouted the friar, hardly

pausing before he delivered the final blow. "To blow upon my horn," gasped the outlaw, and straightway spent his remaining breath upon a blast that filled the air and echoed faintly in the hills around. Hardly had the horn dropped from his fingers when the friar renewed the attack and beat upon the fallen man, whilst Robin parried each blow and prayed the while that help might be near at hand. And, indeed, when Little John arrived with a score or so of archers at his heels he was only just in time. For a moment the friar stood, and, dropping his arm, asked: "Whose be these men?" "Mine," sighed the relieved and wearied man. "Then grant me a boon also, that I may whistle thrice!"

He did so, three long, shrill calls, and from the surrounding woods leaped and jumped a number of huge, fierce-looking hounds, which ran to their master and fawned upon him, jumping up and licking his hands. "A dog for every man of thine and I myself for thee!" exclaimed the friar, who was still eager for Robin's blood.

With one word of command the hounds leapt upon the archers, who fled in fear to the woods, where they climbed trees until Little John gave the word to shoot the dogs. Then a strange and marvellous performance took place. So

well had the beasts been trained that every
one leapt and caught the arrow intended for
its heart in its mouth, and straightway trotted
off and laid the trophy at the master's feet.
Filled with wondering dismay, Little John bade
two archers shoot the same dog. The effect
was instantaneous; each dog aimed at lay with
an arrow in his heart and one between his
teeth.   Fearing the loss of any more of his
beloved animals, the friar loudly cried : "Hold !
Enough !" and submitted himself to Robin, and
inquired his name.

Robin gladly told the friar who and what
he was, and how he guessed who the monk
must be.

"Art thou indeed that Robin Hood ?" won-
deringly exclaimed the friar.   "Many a time
and oft have I heard of thy merry doings, and
if there be no fast days, I'll gladly join thee and
serve thee faithfully as becomes a poor, meek
friar," he ended, in a tone hardly befitting the
words.

Thus did Robin meet his match, and his band
became the richer by Friar Tuck, who turned
out to be a skilled forester and an excellent
cook.

Chapter V

The Sheriff Dines with Robin Hood

SOME time had passed since his encounter with Friar Tuck and Robin was getting just a little bit bored by the uneventful life they had been living. As he trimmed his bow, he kept his eye well on the road, lest perchance he should miss an opportunity for further sport. After a while a butcher passed by on a bonny fine mare, with a large basket full of meat, and evidently bound for Nottingham market. Robin thought of the fun in changing places with the man and seeing once more the life and gaiety at the market, so he accordingly called out: "Good-morrow, good fellow. Hast a basket full of gold there that thou singest so cheerily?"

"Nay, friend," laughed he of the blue smock. "I am only an honest butcher and am on my way to Nottingham market to sell my meat."

Said Robin: "I have a mind to turn butcher also. Wilt sell me thy goods and thy horse?"

"Aye!" laughed the other, thinking Robin

did but jest. "If thou canst give me four silver marks, right gladly art thou welcome to the goods."

"Done!" shouted Robin, in high glee. "Throw in that blue smock of thine, and thy cap, and I'll make it five."

The butcher, seeing the other meant business, and greedily watching the coins as Robin counted them out, quickly snatched the money, and threw off his cap and smock, leaving horse and basket for the other to take possession of them.

Donning the strange attire and mounting the mare occupied only a few minutes, and by-and-by there arrived at the market a new and utterly strange butcher.

So, first putting up his horse at an inn, Robin found an empty stall, and, laying out his stock, began to cry: "Buy! Buy! Who'll buy? Juicy mutton, prime beef! Buy! Buy!"

The first woman who purchased was so amazed at the generous change she received that she quickly told others, and soon a large crowd of women-folk gathered round Robin's stall, each eager to buy. Amongst these was the Sheriff's housekeeper, and she found that for one penny she had received as much as she generally paid five pennies for. So, carrying her purchases, and very well pleased with herself, she hurried home to inform her mistress.

Many a poor widow had cause to bless that young butcher, for not only did he give them their meat cheaply, but he would throw an extra juicy piece in for a very poorly clad woman.

Now the strange butcher quickly sold his stock, and hummed a merry tune as he prepared to pack up. Meanwhile the other butchers eyed him with malice, for not a customer had they served all the morning, and so, as they gathered together to fume and fret, evil whispers were afloat as to the new man.

"Methinks the man is mad," said one. "Surely! he is a prodigal who has come into his lands and property and has chosen thus to fling away his goods," said another. "In any case, he is a daft fellow. Let us invite him to dinner. Perchance he'll pay for us all," said a third. The notion seemed to find favour amongst the others, for they gathered round the new man and eagerly invited him to join them at dinner. Robin accepted, eager for further adventure, and soon found himself at the end of a long table, down which sat all his fellow-tradesmen, and

by his side sat the town Sheriff himself.
Always it fell to the !ot of the visitor to say
grace, so, deepening his voice and lowering
his head, friend Robin recited :

> "Pray God bless us all,
>   And our meat, within this place ;
> A cup of sack so good will nourish our blood,
>   And so do I end my grace."

Without more ado they set to, and large
dishes of freshly boiled meat were brought
in and as quickly vanished down the throats
of the feasters.

Tankards of ale and of sack were placed on
the table and every one helped himself. A right
jovial feast it was, where each ate his fill.

When all had finished, Robin called out for
more wine. "And let it be your best," he
added. "Let us be merry to-day," he said.
"And as this is my first day among you, I'll
pay the reckoning."   This last satisfied the
others, and they drank and drank, and more
than confirmed their suspicions that this was
truly a madman. Whilst quip and joke were
passing between the guests, and the ale was
sparkling in the pewter mugs, the Sheriff took
advantage of the noise and the fellow's seeming
madness to ask Robin if he sold live cattle as
cheaply as he did the joints, thinking he, too,

could drive an excellent bargain with the youngster.

"Aye, indeed that I do!" cried Robin in an eager voice. "Some two or three hundred horned beasts I have ready for sale, and a hundred acres or so of good broad pasture-land. Should it please your worship to see it, come with me this very day and I'll sell at your own price."

With much haste, therefore, and eager to start off, the Sheriff drank a last cup of sack "To our better acquaintance," and winked wickedly over at Robin. Like a wise man, and a crafty one, he took only a bare three hundred pounds in gold, the very least he could offer for *such* cattle and *such* fine land, and this was tied in a bag and fastened in front of his saddle.

Being in an extra good temper, and pleased at the prospect of making his fortune, the Sheriff enlivened the journey recounting tales of his success in business and his civic dignity, laying extra stress upon the fact that with the great Sheriff of the county he was going to lead a party of men against a wicked outlaw known as "Robin Hood," and how, when he caught him, he would "slit his nose and cut off his ears." Listening with proper wonder and awe

"TO OUR BETTER ACQUAINTANCE"

to such boastings and threats, the real Robin gaily set the horses at a fine gallop, pretending to be listening intently to the Sheriff's gossip, but really meditating as to the right punishment for this vainglorious creature.

As they rode through the forest, a hundred head of King's deer trotted nimbly across the road some distance off. "How like you *my* cattle, good Master Sheriff?" inquired the outlaw. "Are they not full, fat and fair?"

The Sheriff shifted restlessly in his saddle. This part of the forest was unknown to him, and they had left all signs of human habitation far behind, and the day was drawing to a close. Besides, after all, was not this man a complete stranger to him? he thought uneasily. Supposing, just supposing, this were a trap and this butcher—— At the very thought the unhappy man tightened his rein and nervously clutched his money-bag. "I like them not," he muttered, in answer to Robin's question. "And I tell thee plainly, I'll go no farther with thee, for I like not thy company!"

Robin laughed long and wickedly, which more than incensed the other. In alarm he pulled the rein to turn his horse round, but Robin jerked it back, and, putting the horn to his lips, forthwith blew a loud and mighty blast upon it. "Thou villain!" roared the Sheriff, mad with fear and anger, and, drawing his sword, would have dealt Robin a deadly blow, but the agile young butcher was used to such tricks and easily evaded the onslaught. Then from the thickets on every side came men all dressed in green, who quickly surrounded the furious citizen, whom they regarded as lawful game for their sport, pinching, teasing, and pricking him, till that worthy was fit to explode with indignation and wrath.

"Escort our guest," commanded Robin. "Know ye not that the Sheriff of Nottingham is to sup with us to-day?" The men fell back and Little John thus welcomed the high guest:

"Thrice welcome, Sir Sheriff, to our festive board. Once for the sake of Robin Hood, our good master, once for thy good fellowship, and once again because thou shalt pay the reckoning."

The Sheriff's doubts had now become certainties, and he miserably realized that he was a prisoner in the hands of this hated outlaw; and as he thought of his gold in the bag and the cattle and lands that would never be his, he groaned feebly and shrank away from their touch. But Little John boldly seized his arm and carried, or rather dragged, the unfortunate man by secret and dark dells through the glade into an open clearing where a large number of men were already sat down and where the smell of a savoury dish greeted their nostrils as they appeared.

The cook, none other than Friar Tuck, his duties now being over, stood at the head of the board and solemnly, amidst a deep silence in which only the rustling leaves could be heard whispering to each other, said his original grace :

> "For what we are about to receive
> May the Sheriff truly pay for.   Amen."

Loud shouts of laughter followed, and, as they sat down, it was the miserable Sheriff who sat in the place of honour and Robin himself who waited upon his every need.   He toyed with his food, and although Robin saw to it that his plate was never empty and his cup always full, the Sheriff made a miserable meal, and was thankful when the others made a movement to rise.   "How should he get home?" was his thought.   "How long would this impudent scoundrel keep him prisoner?   He would send a body of a hundred soldiers to capture him—when he got back—if *ever* he got back," he thought sadly.

Little John had meanwhile taken off his cloak

and laid it under a tree, where he poured out the glittering torrent of gold from the bag and carefully commenced to count it. "Three hundred pounds!" he exclaimed. "The exact cost of this entertainment, Sir Sheriff," and with a wicked gleam of amusement in his eye waited for that crestfallen dignitary to assent. "Alack! Alack!" he whimpered. "Let me go, I pray thee, of thy mercy!" and seizing the opportunity he made as if to escape into the woods behind, but they were too quick for him, and had him blindfold in a trice, and led him, stumbling and cursing, round in a circle, bringing him out once more on the road toward Nottingham, where his horse stood waiting. The outlaws released him and scattered, each in a different direction, whilst the Sheriff made his way slowly home, a sadder, a poorer, but a wiser man.

Chapter VI

How the Bishop Paid the Reckoning

"COME, Friar," said Robin one morning during a sojourn in the Forest of Barnesdale to jolly Friar Tuck. "Prithee, lend me thy gown. Methinketh I will make a likely priest."

Some half-hour later the good friar, greatly intent upon the preparation of that day's food, was genuinely astonished at seeing his leader, with his kirtle drawn high above his knees, running excitedly toward the camp. "Good news, Tuck!" he cried, and forthwith blew upon his horn, whilst at the same moment his men gathered round, all excited and eager to know the cause of the summons.

Then Robin hastily told them how that he had discovered from two strange monks that the stout and pompous Bishop of Hereford was that day to visit his friend and colleague the Right Reverend Bishop of York, and *was to pass through Barnesdale.*

Each nudged his nearest neighbour, and

50

smiled and winked knowingly, until Robin
called two of the outlaws to go shoot a couple
of fine deer and pass them over to Friar Tuck,
who would then roast them whole. "For," concluded Robin, "it minds me to ask the Bishop
to dine with *us* to-day."

"Right willingly will I do my share," returned the cook, his little brown eyes twinkling
merrily. "Was I not two years in his household, and do I not know the tasty bits his heart
delighteth in ?"

Robin now divided his band into four sections,
with a leader over each. Little John and
Allan-a-Dale (who by this time had become a
famous outlaw) commanded two sections, and
Will Stutely and Robin himself led the other
bands. To the leaders he unfolded his plan.
Four roads ran in different directions through
the forest, and as no one knew the exact way
his lordship and company would take, each
section was to take cover at the point where a
road entered the dark and leafy woods. When
the Bishop and his followers made their appearance the leader of the section at that road was
to sound his horn, so that the others might come
up quickly to the place—in case the Bishop's
men should prove troublesome, but principally
to provide an escort for such an important

personage. All were to be disguised as shepherds, wearing loose smocks and wide-brimmed hats.

One section, under Robin himself, killed and skinned a fat buck and hung it over a huge fire of sticks and logs, when the sound of singing was faintly borne to them on the wind. He who was on the look-out quickly gave the word that the Bishop and his party were coming that way, at which news the outlaws began to caper and dance, and piled the fire higher, until the odour of half-cooked venison filled the air around. Meanwhile the Bishop came nearer.

Suddenly he stopped short, and calling his cook (who always travelled in his master's company), he said, sniffing doubtfully at first : "Do I smell venison roasting?" The cook had also perceived the odour, and others, too, ceased their singing and with noses uplifted sniffed the air.

Leaving their horses tethered to trees within easy reach, they crept along on foot, treading only on grassy parts and avoiding all twigs and fallen leaves, till, with a sudden rush and whoop of joy, they burst in upon a few shepherds dancing round the fire, over which swung one of the King's own deer. "This is a clear case," said the Bishop aloud. "Seize the villains!"

The poor shepherds scattered in affright, but they were easily caught and brought back to the

Bishop, where they threw themselves down and begged for mercy.

"Ye rogues!" thundered the prelate. "Know ye not that I am the great Bishop of Hereford, and beg ye mercy from me?" The captives continued on their knees, but he sternly ordered them to get up, and then his men bound them with ropes about their feet and hands.

"Repent if ye can, ye villains," he called to them angrily, "for within a week shall ye all be hanged in a row."

Whilst they were searching for something with which to bind the last man he suddenly drew a horn from beneath his tunic and sounded it. Before the Bishop and his men realized what had happened there was a sound of hurrying feet. From all directions there came pouring in upon the terrified Bishop and his company some forty and five tall, strapping shepherds.

Robin raised his hand and immediately one and all threw off the shepherds' apparel and with a joyous shout stood forth, every man in Lincoln green. The Bishop, thoroughly alarmed, hurried away to his horse, mounted, and would have ridden off, but that a man in green rose, as it seemed, out of the earth, and turned the horse's head, so that he faced the robbers whom he had thought to lead triumphantly into the city of York. He groaned aloud, and trembled so that he almost fell."

"Cheer you, my lord!" cried bold Robin. "Come and dine with us under the greenwood tree," and made as if to assist the good man to alight. But he, kicking aside the hand that would have helped him, and knowing there was no way of escape, ruefully started to dismount. But his legs were yet unsteady, and before he could save himself he had slipped heavily to the ground. All but the Bishop's own company laughed at his sorry plight, till Robin bade two of his own men to lift him and carry him off by dark and winding paths to their lair.

Meanwhile the ropes had been loosed, and the shepherds, who were the primary cause of the prelate's anger, stood free once more, and they, drawing aside those who had bound them, bade them to be off with all speed while there was yet time unless they wanted to be hanged from the forest oaks.

By the time Robin and his band had arrived by a short and secret path the great banquet was already set, and Friar Tuck was well pleased with his own efforts. When the two appeared afar off, still carrying the Bishop, a mighty cheer went up from all the men.

Good Friar Tuck instituted himself chief

butler, and only the choicest and most juicy portions found their way to the Bishop's plate. Robin filled his cup again and again with good red wine, and under the influence of the excellent food and drink the worthy prelate somewhat recovered his equanimity, and began scheming as to how he could escape and carry with him the treasures and gold he was taking as presents to his friend the Archbishop. Being somewhat silent, therefore, whilst the others laughed and joked and told tales, he waited till the feast was over, and then, in his smoothest, silkiest tones he asked : "Master Robin, right well have I enjoyed thy excellent dinner. Tell me, therefore, what I owe, and allow me to proceed upon my way."

Robin nodded to Little John, who gravely asked for his purse. "With all my heart! responded the prelate grandly, flinging his purse to the outlaw. "And should there be anything over, I pray thee give it to the poor."

Amidst silence Little John opened the mouth of the purse and counted out the golden pounds.

"What wealth we have here!" he cried, with a great laugh, and lightly tossed the coins to Allan-a-Dale. "Here! Allan lad. The Bishop bids thee buy ribbons for thy lady."

Robin then directed his men to unload the Bishop's pack-mules.

Spreading a broad length of cloth upon the grass, Little John unfolded a heap of treasures before the eyes of them all, for this was the spoil to be divided amongst themselves, so eagerly they watched as each chose his share.

By now the Bishop was frantic with rage and disappointment, wringing his hands and wailing with grief. "Give me back my goods and let me go," he implored. "Not so!" cheerfully responded Robin. "Art thou not commanded to give to the poor?"

But his troubles were not yet over, for up jumped Robin. "Allan!" said he sharply, "my heart misgives me that our honoured guest is sad, therefore do thou give us a lively, merry tune and we will dance dull care away."

Thereupon Allan began to play a lively tune upon his pipe and, the others beginning to dance, Robin dragged the Bishop upon his feet, and half encircling his stout partner with one arm, and pulling him round with the other, the poor man was whirled round and round to a right joyous caper.

For a long time the dance went on, every one enjoying himself except the prelate.

Chapter VII

Concerning Sir Richard of the Lea

"**N**OW what sorry scarecrow is this?" asked Little John of the outlaws gathered round him. "'Look not upon the outward appearance lest ye be deceived' saith the proverb, and so our sorry friend upon a sorrier steed shall be our guest to-day."

The horseman was dressed as a knight, but his clothes, which were old and extremely shabby, hung loosely upon him. His visor was pulled down over his eyes and his head was sunk upon his breast. One foot held the stirrup limply, whilst the other hung dejectedly down.

"A sorrier man than he was one
Ne'er rode on a summer's day."

The poor lean beast on which he ambled was a picture of misery as it wearily shuffled along the road.

"Now, by Our Lady!" said honest John, moved with pity, "ne'er saw I a man more downcast," and running out into the wood he thus addressed the knight:

57

"A happy day to you, good Sir Knight. Behold! my master awaits your gracious company at meat this day."

"Nay, good fellow," gently returned he. "I am full of trouble and in no mood for feasting. Yet would I thank thy master for his courtesy toward a broken man."

"A broken man!" cheerily responded the tall outlaw. "All the more welcome then to our camp."

"Who is this master of thine?" inquired the knight. "Robin Hood!" cried Little John, with proper pride. "An' if thou tellest thy woes to him, maybe he can help thee."

"I think not, good friend," returned he sadly. "But gladly will I dine with such a famous host." "Away to the camp!" called Little John to the others.

Robin stepped forward to greet the newcomer, and doffing his cap and bowing low he gave the knight a hearty welcome. Robin waited on him and heaped his plate and replenished his goblet, but still the guest remained silent. Dinner over, he made a short speech, thanking them one and all for the right royal way in which he had dined, and turned, aside to Little John to thank him for his thoughtful attention to his steed. Then he made as if to depart, but Robin hailed him, saying:

"Good Sir Knight, 'tis always a custom with us to feast a guest well and then to make a speedy reckoning. Bring hither his money-bags."

"No! No!" cried the other. "I beg of you not to shame me. I have in this world but mine honour and ten silver shillings," and again his head drooped dejectedly.

But Little John had already untied the bags, and in the one he found a part of a loaf and in the other a cloak. Unrolling this, he found therein a piece of linen, and tied tightly inside this were ten silver shillings.

"The knight speaks true," gravely announced he. "Ten shillings is the total sum." "Half of it will suffice for the meal," said Robin, with compassion. "Sir Knight, how came you in such sorry plight?"

Then he told them. He had a son, a stalwart young fellow of some twenty summers. Unfortunately he had killed a man in fair fight, but the friends of the dead man refused all overtures of peace and sought to have the lad publicly hanged. Finally they had taken the case to the Law Courts, and it was there decreed that unless four hundred pounds was immediately forthcoming

the young man must die. To procure this
enormous sum of money the father had mort-
gaged his broad lands and cattle, his castle also,
and everything of value that he had, to the
Abbot of St Mary's Abbey. The lawyers had
been merciful and given him twelve months
wherein to raise the money, whilst his son
lingered and pined in a dark and unwholesome
dungeon. The very next day was the last that
was left of the twelve months, and he had not
nearly gathered the four hundred pounds together, so he was on his way to the Abbot to
beg a further year of grace. The sad tale told,
he turned away his head that they might not
see his tears.

"Let me be your friend," begged Robin, in
his masterful way. "I pray you to accept of
me the loan of four hundred pounds. Nay,
thank me not," added he hurriedly, as Sir
Richard in broken accents would have spoken
his gratitude. "You have but changed
creditors. Natheless I trust you will not find
me so harsh as this most un-Christian Abbot."

Forthwith he ordered several of the men to
run to the store and bring out the richest cloths,
and Little John was told to measure three yards
of each and give them to the knight, and as
that good fellow measured with his bow and

gave one yard extra in every three, soon a
goodly pile of costly material was waiting.
One of their own horses was brought round,
with gay trappings of leather and silver, for the
knight's own use, and the cloth was placed in neat
bundles upon the back of a second, whilst doublet
and hose, with a cloak to match, were fitted
upon Sir Richard, and Little John added a pair
of finely worked leather boots with gilt spurs.
"The owner having no further use for them,"
he explained, with a sly wink, so that when the
knight rode a few paces off he was admired by
them all, such a splendid figure he looked.
Before he turned to depart he wheeled round,
and holding his naked sword upright in the air
cried :

"Good Master Robin Hood, and you his
merry men! sadness filled my heart when I
rode through the forest, but you have turned it
into joy and gladness, and from the fullness of
my gratitude I thank you. Farewell! This day
twelvemonth I will return and repay my debt.
I swear it by my sword, and Sir Richard of the
Lea never yet broke faith." So saying, he raised
the hilt and kissed it solemnly, and then with
a flourish and a clash as it clanked into the
sheath he put spurs to his horse and galloped
off.

"Ho! Sir Knight, stop a moment," came
in a deep round voice, and Friar Tuck, with his
cooking apron all flying in the breeze, came
running up at a break-neck speed and gave his
steel helmet into the knight's hand. It was the
envy of every man who saw it, being of finest
metal with a delicate tracery of gold wrought
upon the front. With a courteous acknowledg-
ment the rider accepted the gift and set it upon
his head, and once more galloped off into the
silent darkness of the forest.

Now the Abbot never dreamed that the
knight could pay, and, being anxious to hold
those fair pastures as his own, he had bidden a
number of guests to feast with him that very
night and revelry and song filled the sacred
precincts of the old abbey. Suddenly a loud
and impatient knocking was heard at the outer
gate. Pushing his way past the doorkeeper and
through the line of guests, in strode Sir Richard,
splendidly attired, and followed by ten retainers
whom he had picked up on his way. Now he
was resolved to put the pretended benevolence of
the Abbot to the test. Dropping on one knee
and holding his cap of steel in his hand, he
bowed low before the astonished Abbot, saying:
"Sir Abbot, the crops have failed, the winter
has been severe, and yesterday morning found

me with but ten silver shillings. Give me grace, therefore, for another year, and surely I will pay thee with double interest."

"Never a day!" roared the Abbot. "Did not the agreement say one twelvemonth, and does not the time expire this very day? No grace shalt thou have from me, but as surely as the morning light shall come, so surely shall thy fair lands be taken from thee, aye, and thy castle and all that thou hast, as saith the agreement, for the Church doth ever administer the law." Then he continued: "Away from my presence, thou false knight. How darest enter without money to redeem thy bond?"

Springing to his feet the knight exclaimed angrily: "Thou it is who art false, churlish priest! No land of mine shall Church or abbey have, and, so saying, he raised his hand, and two of the servants drew near, carrying a large leathern bundle. This they opened and poured out the four hundred pounds upon the table.

The Abbot was now compelled to give up the bond, and Sir Richard received it without another word. Then he and his men strode out of the hall and into the night, and turned homeward.

Right sorrowfully came his good lady to meet

him, but with a joyous shout he waved the
bond aloft, and hurriedly told her the story.
Then arm in arm in joyful thankfulness they
entered the castle, which, thanks to Robin
Hood, was saved from the grasp of an avaricious
Abbot.

Chapter VIII

Reynold Greenleafe

THE Sheriff of Nottingham has offered a young bullock as a prize at the shooting match next fair-day. Wilt try, Little John?" asked Robin of his henchman. "Who's competing?" inquired he. On learning that a certain boastful forester who was well hated by all the outlaws had entered, Little John expressed his willingness to shoot a shaft or two for the credit of the band.

The morning dawned sunny and fair, and as soon as the stall-holders had spread their wares for sale a tall and ungainly beggar strolled into the grounds, and after having had his name entered for the shooting, wandered idly round, gazing at the various side-shows with very little interest, until he came near a platform raised slightly off the ground, where a stout man with a very red and bull-like neck stood twirling a quarter-staff round his head.

"Come up, my masters, come up and taste the quality of a lad from Lincoln," shouted he.

A large crowd had gathered round, and, judging by the silence, they did not seem eager to test the prowess of this burly champion. Little John pressed nearer the stage. Here he learned that several young men had stepped up for a fair and friendly bout, but each had returned in a few moments with bleeding head, or arms or ribs bruised with hard blows. Even as he listened yet another youth stepped boldly to the front and upon the platform, exclaiming with a broad grin at the audience: "Crack my skull an thou canst!" Blows waxed hard and swift for a few moments, and all was hubbub and noise, and then—silence. The young hothead was knocked out. Left by himself, and with another victory to add to his long list, the champion strutted up and down, a look of intense satisfaction glowing upon his face, whilst he bowed and smirked and preened himself even as a slightly ruffled peacock would do. Tiring of this, and seeing the crowd begin to melt, he began to address scornful remarks to the bystanders, declaring that not one was man enough to try another bout with him. Amused by his vanity, and itching to strip his conceit from him, Little John burst out in a rude and noisy laugh.

The champion instantly took offence and

threatened to beat the beggar's jacket if his manners did not improve. "I be but a poor beggar, but I'll save thee *that* trouble," grinned the giant, whereupon he leapt lightly upon the the wooden platform. Directly he raised his staff many voices shouted: "Strike a blow for Nottingham, lad." This in truth he did, and many a one followed it. At first the man from Lincoln tried to beat him down by sheer force, but Little John had seen that trick before and easily parried the blows, and now the pair went round and round the platform, the crowd roaring excitedly and following the man from Nottingham with eager eyes.

Never before had a man stood up so long before the champion from Lincoln, and angry at his opponent's skill, and fearful lest he should be beaten to his knees, the champion struck out wildly, and, losing his temper, he dealt desperately heavy blows. It took Little John all his skill to evade these, but, watching his chance, he got in one crashing stroke upon his opponent's right shoulder, and then another mighty blow upon the head. The champion of Lincoln rolled over and lay very still. "Go brag in Lincoln of how thou didst meet a Nottingham man," laughed the victor, and not one out of the crowd that had gathered round but had a

cheer and smile for Little John, a clap on his
back, or else a handshake.

Thinking of the most important contest of
the day, he hurriedly adjusted his tattered
coat and made haste to the butts. But he
had not been shooting for many minutes when
he was recognized by a knot of onlookers as
the Nottingham champion with the quarter-
staff, and in less time than it takes to tell a
great crowd gathered round and eagerly followed
every shot. To their huge delight he was as
skilful with his bow as with his staff, and soon
all the competitors except the boastful forester
and Little John had retired crestfallen.

Casting disdainful looks upon this unknown
beggar who dared to rival him in archery, the
forester loudly called for a willow wand, saying:
"Give me a man's mark; any child could hit
yonder bull." They brought a wand, but Little
John exclaimed: "Peel the wand and set it
one hundred yards beyond the target!" This
was done, whilst the crowd murmured excitedly
and wished their hero luck. When all was
ready the forester made careful preparations to
shoot first, and, taking a long and steady aim,
he shot. The silence was broken, and tongues
wagged, and a few murmurings were heard, but
above all a long and scornful laugh rang out,

LITTLE JOHN BEATS THE CHAMPION FROM LINCOLN

for the arrow had whistled by the wand and buried itself in earth a few yards behind. The forester turned aside that none might see his deep annoyance, whilst Little John fitted his arrow with more than his usual preciseness, and lightly loosed his shaft. This time the silence was broken by a ringing cheer, for the wand was split down the centre. The Sheriff was sent for, and condescended to ride right up to the mark to see there was no mistake. Quickly he returned to Little John and said: "Beggar, thou art indeed the best shot I have ever seen. I declare thou art winner of my prize. What is thy name, and whence come ye?"

"I am called Reynold Greenleafe, and from no one place do I come, but go wandering round, seeking to improve my fortune."

"Thou art a likely fellow," returned the Sheriff. "If thou wilt enter my service, thou shalt have good food and plenty of fine clothes, and twenty shillings a year."

Thinking it would look suspicious to refuse such a noble offer, Reynold consented, and followed the Sheriff to his house.

For a while all went well. The situation suited him excellently, and, as there was plenty to eat and nothing to do, Reynold was really

quite happy with his new lot. But a quarrel
arose because the butler declared he was a lazy
fellow and should be made to work for his
meals, especially as he ate as much as ten
servants. Now one morning after the Sheriff
had gone out hunting Reynold still lay abed.
Hour after hour, till after noon, he lay
sleeping; but at last he arose and, feeling very
empty, he made his way straight to the pantry
in order to feast himself. But alas! there at
the door stood his enemy, who roughly asked
him where he was going. "To the pantry to
break my fast," answered simple Reynold.
"Thou lazy villain!" roared the butler. "No
meat till thou hast worked for it. Clean all the
silver, every jot of it, and when thou hast
finished maybe I'll give thee a little food."
Reynold said nothing, but made as if to brush
past into the pantry, when the butler turned
and with a snick! the door was locked and
Reynold and his triumphant enemy left outside.

"Hurry! do thy work first," commanded the
butler. A terrific buffet which bowled the
lesser man over was Reynold's reply, and
screaming the terrified butler fled to the kitchen.
A kick opened the pantry door, and in another
moment Master Reynold was regaling himself
with a large pasty and a bottle of the Sheriff's

best wine. He was not left long undisturbed, for down the passage strode the cook, followed at a safe distance by the still scared butler. "Oh ho!" blustered the cook. "What dost thou here, Greenleafe?" "Hast eyes?" curtly inquired Reynold. "I am dining. Wilt join me? Come! drink the Sheriff's health in his best red wine!"

"Thou impudent rogue," cried the enraged cook, and drawing the short dagger that always hung by his side he made as if to stab him. But Reynold was not slow, and, dashing down his pasty, he unsheathed his hunting-knife and was ready for the fight. Out of the larder and up and down the big room did these two fight, their weapons clashing harshly, so that the poor butler fled affrighted to the cellar. For nearly sixty minutes they strove together, but in the end they called a truce, and Reynold, perceiving that a good fighter was going to waste in the Sheriff's household, asked if he would care to join Robin Hood's band of merry men. "What sayst thou? Change the Sheriff's service for ours. We'll dress thee in Lincoln green and show thee the free life of the merry greenwood men."

"Willingly will I," replied the cook. "Often have I longed for a change. Yea, I'll come."

The two then shook hands and drank their late master's health in a bottle of sparkling Burgundy.

"Truly," mused Reynold, "my conscience pricks me sorely in that of late I have neglected the Sheriff's plate. Surely, now, we will take it with us to Master Robin, and when I present thee, thou shalt present the plate." So, with much chuckling, and there being no one to stay their hands, they seized every piece of silver and gold and stuffed them into an old sack, and then, thumping it up and down on the floor, and after making a terrible clatter, whereby the quaking butler must think the fight was still proceeding, they quickly left the house and made toward Sherwood.

Chapter IX

Robin Quarrels with Little John and is Captured by the Sheriff

WHAT is the matter with our master?" asked Little John of Will Stutely one fine morning. "Of late he looketh worn and haggard, and his temper, which was ever hot, is almost unbearable just now."

"I know not, John," was the reply. "Methinketh he struggles against a sickness. Why, 'twas only the other day he did threaten to dismiss me from the band, and for what reason, think ye? Only that I sang a right merry stave as I tended to my bow. God grant he soon be restored to his merry self again."

"And so say I," said the big outlaw. "But here he cometh himself. Look ye, Will! Is it not sad to see our master so downcast?"

Slowly toward them came Robin.

"I'm sick even to death of this life!" he exclaimed peevishly. "I'll stand it no more. I'll to Nottingham and perchance there I'll find some adventure which may carry off my gloom. Well, blockheads! are ye dumb? Did I not speak? What think ye?" he snapped out to his two well-tried friends.

"Nay, master," answered Little John, in a gentle voice, "thou art not well. Come, lie down awhile, and when thou art rested we'll go down into Nottingham together and make merry there."

"Doddering old woman that thou art! Knowest thou not that I was never sounder in health than now? I'll to Nottingham—by myself."

"Even so," replied John. "And Will and I will surely go with thee, for thou art not thyself to-day."

"What!" roared Robin. "Said I not that I would go alone? Hold thy tongue, man."

"That will I. Natheless, thou art not fit to go alone, and we go with thee," stubbornly returned the unruffled giant.

"Ho!" hotly returned Robin. "Am *I* captain or thou?"

"Surely *thou* art. But give up thy trip to town for this day," pleaded Little John.

"I'll be thwarted no longer. Stand aside!" roared the leader. But Little John moved not an inch.

"Out of my way, I say!" bellowed the infuriated Robin, and seeing the other made no attempt to move, blind with rage, he raised his hand and struck him full across the face.

"Now thou hast gone too far," said Little John sadly. "Guard thyself!"

But his new-born anger died almost as soon as it was kindled, as, glancing at his leader, he saw the careworn lines that made the face look old, and, dropping his staff, he burst out sorrowfully:

"Robin Hood, I never thought thou wouldst have struck me in anger. I strike not a sick man. But Little John will be thy man no more," and turning abruptly on his heel he strode off into the forest. With never a glance at Will Stutely, Robin Hood took the road to Nottingham, but Will followed after him, at a discreet distance, though Robin knew not of it.

Robin's anger passed like a sudden summer storm, and sorrowfully musing over his own childish display of temper he slowly pursued his way and at length reached the town. There, with humiliated heart and mind, he entered a church, and, kneeling beside the altar, he was soon absorbed in meditation and prayer.

Now one of the monks, who owed Robin a grudge because once Robin had relieved him of a goodly purse, chanced to recognize the outlaw, and, quietly locking the door, he ran off at full speed to tell the Sheriff, who at once sent off a strong guard to surround the building. The priest then stealthily unlocked the door, and, peering in, discovered the outlaw in pious attitude exactly as he had left him.

He then signalled to the guard that their quarry was still unaware of his plight.

His meditations over, Robin rose up from the altar in a chastened frame of mind, repentant that he had struck such a worthy friend as Little John, and determined to go back at once and seek him and make amends. As a penance he himself would no more lead the band, but would serve as lieutenant to Little John. With his mind full of these thoughts, he made his way with bent head through the church and entered the porch. A shrill whistle sounded, and Robin, startled out of his reverie, looked up to find himself hemmed in by a number of soldiers.

Realizing his danger, he instantly drew sword and backed to the wall, where he fought desperately, but against hopeless odds. Bitterly thinking of the escort he had so ungraciously refused, Robin fought long and fiercely, until at length he fell exhausted and wounded, when the others rushed upon him and haled him off at once to the prison, shouting and calling as they went along that the famous outlaw was captured at last.

Arrived at the prison, he was chained with heavy fetters and flung into the deepest dungeon, so far beneath the ground that never did the light of day shine in this cell.

As the great iron door clanked behind him, Robin, with just enough sense left to realize that this must indeed be his end, lapsed back into merciful unconsciousness.

Whilst all this commotion was taking place, Will Stutely, who had seen enough to make him alarmed for the life of his master, fled in hot haste back to the camp. Once within its precincts, he sounded such a blast upon his horn that the sound penetrated even unto the remotest parts of the forest. Little John heard it as, with pack on his pack, he was preparing to quit the camp for ever.

Seeing him go off in the opposite direction, Will ran to him: "Come back," he implored. "Robin Hood, sore wounded, is taken by the Sheriff, and must surely die unless we rescue him. Forget thy quarrel and help us."

"By my faith, indeed I will," heartily responded the noble-hearted giant, all his love for his leader overwhelming his heart now that he knew he was in danger and needed help.

All the band had now gathered round and demanded to know the cause of the imperative summons, and carefully Will Stutely told them. With fierce, wild cries they bade Little John at once to lead them against the city, and they would fight to the death for their leader's freedom. But Little John commanded them to wait till they had a plan of deliverance prepared.

"Do ye prepare your bows and swords for battle, whilst Will and I go to Nottingham," said he, and so these two staunch friends, hurriedly garbing themselves as strolling friars, made off at great speed toward the town, whilst the camp, alive with indignation, was sharpening swords and re-stringing bows.

Nearing the city, they saw two monks galloping along at a high speed. Little John stood directly in their path and held up his hands that they should stop. "Delay us not," cried the leader of the two, "for we are messengers to the King!"

"Might two humble friars ask if it be good news that ye take to his Majesty?" inquired Will.

"Good news indeed," cried the monk, swelling

with pride, and reining in his steed. "Know ye not that the bold outlaw Robin Hood is now captured and the credit is mine—*mine*? I did it. The rogue is laid by the heels, and in three days, when I shall have returned from the King, perchance with many honours for myself and the Sheriff, he is to be hanged on a high gibbet in the market-place!"

"Never shalt thou return to cause the death of the truest man that ever lived," roared Little John, and, drawing sword, he killed the monk at a blow. Binding the other trembling monk, they returned to the camp, where for two days there was great preparation of the King's uniform from the fine cloth in their store.

On the morning of the third day the Sheriff's watchman saw a large company of stalwart men marching toward the city. Recognizing the King's uniform, he at once ran to his master and told his news. Now the Sheriff, filled with hopes of high honour and reward for this magnificent capture, hastily donned his finest apparel and with dignity and patience waited the arrival of the royal guests.

With a martial air the company all passed, and halted outside the residence of the Sheriff. Stepping forward, the captain bowed low and said:

"The King sends thee greeting, Sir Sheriff, and would thank thee, for at last thou hast rid the country of that pestilent rogue, Robin Hood. Thy messenger he keeps with him, that he may show him great honour, and has sent me, the captain of his guard, with my men to assist thee should any attempt at rescue be made."

Right eager was the Sheriff to attend to the wants of the royal guests, and leaving his men comfortably settled before a large dinner, the captain sat at the Sheriff's own table. A splendid feast was served, and in his desire to be hospitable the Sheriff drank more than was good for him, and the captain also appeared to be in his cups.

"Where keep ye this rogue?" innocently inquired the captain of the Sheriff, who chuckled and winked wickedly as he leaned over and whispered: "In the darkest dungeon—thirty feet below the ground." "Methinks I should like a view of the rascal; and yet," murmured the captain half to himself, "I have heard he is a desperate fellow."

Up jumped the Sheriff, made brave by the large quantity of wine he had consumed.

"There is no risk, Captain," he vaunted. "Come, I myself will show thee the fellow."

Calling for torches, the two left the table and moved in the direction of the prison.

"Now do I love thee for a valiant man," exclaimed the captain. "But, I pray thee, give me leave to take six of my men as a guard for us."

"As thou wilt," agreed the Sheriff grandly, remembering the heavy fetters that bound the robber.

The prison gates reached, the head jailer handed his bunch of keys to the Sheriff.

"Sir Sheriff," interposed the captain again, "I do believe *thy* brave spirit has entered into me. Surely, we will leave my men here, and thou and I will carry our own torches. But art sure he is in irons?" he added hastily, as though with some fear.

"Come, Sir Captain," encouraged the Sheriff, becoming bolder as the other seemed to grow more frightened, "trust thyself to my care, and I'll show thee the beauty." Lighting his own torch with unsteady fingers, the Sheriff proceeded down the dark stone steps and along narrow, evil-smelling passages, with the tall captain close behind and apparently quite reassured since the Sheriff had become so bold.

At last they reached a door, all black and studded with iron nails, and this the Sheriff unlocked and with some difficulty pushed open. Peering into the darkness, he called out gloatingly :

"Where *art* thou, friend Robin? Come into the light ; a friend would see thee."

"Truly, Robin, a friend would see thee," roared a familiar voice, and the captain, no other than Little John, seized the Sheriff by the neck and shook him like a rat, then flung him heavily to the floor, where he lay stunned.

Stooping, the tall outlaw unfastened his girdle and took the keys therefrom, and after a little fumbling the fetters fell off from Robin's feet and hands and once more he stood free.

"Little John," said Robin slowly, "three days ago I struck thee and I have repented me ever since. If we ever reach the greenwood again, I declare to you that henceforward I will be your true man."

"Not so, Robin," said John simply ; "I love thee, and I am ever your man. Whatever is past is forgotten. Here's my hand on't."

Silently the two men gripped hands, and never again had they an angry word.

Little John then told of his plan of escape. How that six men stood at the prison gate awaiting orders and that by now ninety more were without the city gates with horses. "They do but await us. But thou must leave this cell as the Sheriff."

Quickly they stript the unconscious Sheriff of his costly robes and threw Robin's tunic over him, fastened him in chains and locked the dungeon door.

And now the Sheriff and the captain proceeded back to the prison gates, where the jailer was told to take great care of the prisoner, and to hold no converse with him, on penalty of his own life. Handing the keys back, the whilom Sheriff gravely took his leave and departed with the captain of the King's guard, the six soldiers following behind.

Some time later the keeper of the city gate was aroused. "The Sheriff would see you," said his man.

"Good keeper," said the Sheriff, "my guest and I have a whim to ride in the moonlight."

"What mad prank is this?" muttered the sleepy gatekeeper, as he opened the gates. "And how can eight men ride without a single horse?"

"Thank you, good fellow," said the Sheriff, as the party leisurely passed through. "Sit not up for us, but get thee back to bed."

The party lost no time in reaching the shelter

of the trees, and Robin received a great welcome from all his men.

Next day there was a great turmoil in the town, for the Sheriff could nowhere be found, and, half crazy with grief and anxiety, his good dame ran about the streets.

It was not until late at night that the poor man was discovered, and when the citizens heard how he had been caught in his own trap, their concern for his safety was turned to laughter at his discomfiture, and many are the rhymes that tell how the Sheriff of Nottingham caught Robin Hood and spent a night in his deepest dungeon.

Hearing that the captain of the guard and the Sheriff had taken a moonlight ride—and without horses, as the dazed gatekeeper persisted—Will Stutely knew that all was clear and Robin safe; so, gathering his men, he went off in a great hurry.

Thus was Robin rescued from the gibbet and cured of his sickness.

Chapter X

The Saving of Will Stutely

THE morning following the camp was all astir as soon as day broke. Will Stutely and four other reckless young outlaws were ordered to buy meal and provender at the market, and, notwithstanding their adventure of the previous evening, they anticipated having some sport.

Late in the evening they returned, but without Will. Sorely injured, with clothes torn to rags, the outlaws had painfully crawled back to the camp.

Sadly they told their tale: how they were quietly going the round of the stalls when some fellow recognized them and instantly raised the alarm. He was a sheriff's officer, and had a dozen or more men at his bidding, and so in a moment they were surrounded, and the Sheriff himself joined the throng, urging his men to set upon the outlaws.

Nothing loath, and surprised into instant action, they had faced the men courageously, and with splendid play of sword and staff fought a passage inch by inch to the gates of the city, leaving a trail of broken heads in their wake. All went well until the very gates were reached, when Will Stutely fell headlong with an arrow through his leg. In a trice he was pounced on and securely bound hand and foot. His companions turned back and fought desperately to rescue him; but all to no purpose, for the odds were heavily against them. Nothing was left to them but flight, so they took to their heels and fled for their very lives, outstripped the Sheriff's men, and had reached the camp in this sorry condition.

The chief outlaw meditated for a while, and then, calling Little John to him, he unfolded a scheme. Little John was to take every available man, and each was to be dressed differently from the others. They were to wander in pairs or singly into the town and thence to the market-place.

"I fear," remarked Robin, "Master Sheriff will remember my recent escape and that he will probably hang poor Will this very day. Now, hark ye! I'll go to town disguised as a beggar. Have thy men sprinkled about amongst the crowd, and look out for me, and keep thine ears open for the sound of my horn.

Should ill befall me and I cannot reach thee, do thou and thy men set upon the guard and rescue Will at all costs."

An hour later a little old man, bent almost double with age, hobbled slowly through the gates of the city.

Scarce had he entered when three coarse soldiers seized upon the old man and brought him before the Sheriff.

Now the Sheriff was much perplexed over the hanging of the outlaw, for, though he had sworn he should hang that very day, he could nowhere find a man willing to do the deed.

For, indeed, the townspeople knew that Robin Hood's vengeance would be swift and sudden, and no man had a wish to lose his life to oblige the Sheriff. So the hours sped by and still the hangman was not found. It was whilst in this dilemma that the Sheriff ordered his soldiers to bring in the first strange beggar they met.

"Fellow," said the Sheriff to the old man, "wilt earn five golden crowns?"

"Aye, good master, right willingly," quavered the ancient.

"Wilt hang a man?" questioned the other doubtfully.

"Two! an you pay me for it," returned the other in thin but eager tones.

"One man at a time," laughed the other savagely. "But he is one of Robin Hood's gang of robbers." Then, throwing a contemptuous look round which included all his own soldiers, he added : "But perhaps thou art afraid also?"

"Not I," murmured the old man. "Robin Hood himself cannot scare me."

"Take him away and feed him," commanded the Sheriff, and the old man was led away to the kitchen.

At a given signal the prison gates opened and allowed a rude open cart to pass through. A strong guard went before and another brought up the rear; in it, seated listlessly with hands tied behind, was Will Stutely, and with him a priest.

Just as the procession reached the foot of the gallows the Sheriff stepped forward with the hangman. Now this man was bleeding profusely about the face, for some one had cast a stone at him with good aim, hearing that he was to hang the outlaw, which showed that the people admired and respected Robin Hood and his merry men and would not willingly harm them.

"Where is thy master now?" sneered the Sheriff. "Hiding like a rabbit in his warren. Methinks young Master Robin is afraid to risk his coward's hide to save his servant."

"Thou vain braggart!" returned Will stoutly. "Know this, when Robin Hood hears of my death there will be a new Sheriff of Nottingham, for he never deserted any of his followers, no! nor ever will," he concluded proudly.

The crowd heard the reply and cheered the resolute outlaw. Then, because he was young and the world was fair to look upon, he called quickly to the hangman:

"Come, fellow, do thy work! If die I must, let it be quickly!"

Slowly, and with his stiff old limbs hampered by his long cloak, the hangman climbed up the steps and stood on the narrow platform with the prisoner. Then, under pretence of tightening the bonds round his wrists, the hangman quickly whipped a knife from under his cloak and with one stroke Will was free. Then, to the amazement of the onlookers, the hangman's back became straight, and off went his long cloak, while they saw him push his knife into the hands of the prisoner, and, drawing his sword, which he had cunningly concealed in the cloak, he stood on the edge of the platform and gazed down on the sea of faces.

" 'Tis Robin Hood himself !" roared a dozen voices at once, and others took up the cry, till all that vast throng shouted wildly for joy.

Peering anxiously amongst the faces nearest him, Robin perceived one burly man clad in a butcher's smock. Then did he blow a cheerful note upon his horn, whereupon some ninety stalwart men steadily forced their way through the throng and right up to the gallows. There they quickly formed themselves into a strong guard under the orders of the burly butcher, whilst Robin and Will stood in their midst.

"Fifty pounds to the man who kills Robin Hood!" shouted the Sheriff, with tears of rage and mortification rolling down his face, whilst the soldiers stood stolidly by, not daring to move a hand, because of Robin's strong band of men. The first blow that was struck, however, cast off the momentary spell, and there immediately ensued a lively struggle, in which the Sheriff and his men, Robin Hood and Little John, ninety outlaws and the crowd were all engaged. The big butcher was merrily cracking heads with a huge club when he perceived the Sheriff feebly parrying the blows of an outlaw, so he turned and would have beaten him to

the earth with one blow, but Robin stepped
between, saying, and smiling too : "Hold, Little
John ! Wouldst not even leave me the Sheriff?"
So, with a happy grin, the giant turned away,
and, clearing a path with his club, was soon
breaking pates where the fight was thickest.

"Thinkest thou *still* that Robin Hood would
desert a friend?" shouted Robin tauntingly,
and with a strong blow with the flat of his
sword he brought the Sheriff to his knees.

Now the Sheriff was a wily man, and knew
that if he stood up he was liable to be beaten
down again, but so long as he remained on his
knees an honourable foe would not hurt him,
so on his knees, with tears of self-pity rolling
down his cheeks, he whined for mercy.

Now close by the market-place was a muddy
ditch, and Robin called Little John and Will.
"Look ye !" said he. "Saw ye ever such a
craven? Give me a hand with him to yonder
ditch."

Howling with fear, and writhing like a slippery
eel, they half dragged, half carried the wretched
man to the brink and there pitched him in.
The stagnant water was but three inches deep,
but underneath was a foot or more of soft black
mud.

Little John lightly leapt to the other side

and a right merry game began. With their long staves the three outlaws poked and smote and rolled the unhappy man back again into the filth, until such a sight as he presented you had never seen before. At last they tired of their new sport, and, allowing the shivering and dirty creature to crawl out, they joined in the laughter and gibes of the citizens and followed him till he crept in at his own door.

Whilst this game was in progress the ninety outlaws had continued the fight with the Sheriff's men and, having soundly thrashed them, were proudly marching through the streets of the city.

Chapter XI

Sir Richard Repays his Debt

FOR the past twelve months Sir Richard of the Lea had tried hard to raise the money wherewith to repay Robin Hood. So he informed all his tenants and farmers of the goodness and generosity of Robin, so that they grew to love that brave young outlaw and swore to help Sir Richard pay his debt, for one and all loved their overlord with an exceeding great love.

All that summer the sun shone strongly and the harvest exceeded all their expectations.

Keeping just enough grain and produce for their own needs, every man sent the surplus to market and turned the produce into hard cash.

Then they chose the oldest greybeard amongst them, who had known Sir Richard since he was a babe, and, having filled a bag with all their monies, they bade him take this gold to the castle and present it to their lord.

Once there, he was quickly admitted into the presence of Sir Richard.

"Master," said the old man feebly, but with an undeniable ring of joy in his quavering tones, "I am no man of words, but we, your faithful servants, do beseech you to take this gold in return for your many kindnesses to us."

Placing the bag upon a table near by, the old farmer would have withdrawn, but that Sir Richard stepped down and took him by the arm and led him back to the table, saying:

"Good Diccon, I thank thee and all thy fellows too. But thou must first sit to dinner with us, and afterward we will see what is in the bag."

So saying, the knight led his humble guest into the dining-hall, never thinking how great was the gift that lay upon his table; but all the same a great peaceful joy crept into his heart as he thought of the good will of his tenants in contributing their share toward the big debt.

After a hearty repast, at which the farmer found himself an honoured guest, he was placed by Sir Richard in the seat of honour, when the bag of money was brought in and opened.

Rightly amazed was the lord of the manor to see the golden coins tumbling out, and when they had counted eight hundred his heart was so moved with tender gratitude toward his men for their practical show of love that he gently but warmly thanked the messenger, exclaiming in broken tones:

"Know—Diccon—a friend of mine—a squire, hath given me money to pay my debt—but now will I return it—and Robin Hood shall know how my tenants—nay—my own dear friends— have rallied round me in my need."

"Ye be right welcome, my lord," answered Diccon. "And know yet this, that never a man of us but would give his life, if need be, for our good lord Sir Richard of the Lea."

So saying, he was dismissed, and many kind words and happy smiles followed him as he hobbled slowly out. It was indeed a proud and happy man that returned to his brethren, and they, hearing of Sir Richard's deep gratitude, were all mightily pleased, for it is indeed true that a good master maketh good servants.

Now all these events took place a month before Sir Richard was due at Robin Hood's camp, and during the next four weeks the castle was thronged with workmen.

One hundred beautiful bows of the true yew-tree were fashioned, and wonderful quivers, all richly carved, were filled with arrows fitted with peacocks' feathers and tipped with silver. Nor did the knight forget the friar and Little John, for a wondrous cap of steel mounted with gold and a pair of finely wrought spurs did he take for these open-hearted fellows. For the leader himself Richard had procured a true Toledo blade of wonderful suppleness, the hilt of which was studded with diamonds and rubies and other precious stones.

The morning chosen for departure found everything ready, and with a light heart the good knight and a hundred men-at-arms, all dressed in gay uniforms of red and white, trooped through the castle gates and took the road for Sherwood.

Some half a mile farther along the road the company was met by the farmers, with Diccon at their head. He was leading a handsome chestnut mare, and desired that Sir Richard would take it as a gift to Robin Hood.

"With all my heart," responded the knight heartily, and he caused the money-bags to be placed upon the charger. Then amidst the cheers and good will of all his tenants the knight and his company slowly rode past and were presently out of sight.

On their way they had to pass the town of Mansfield, and there, just outside a hamlet, they saw a wrestling match was in progress.

Halting his men, the knight, who dearly loved all manner of sport, watched for a time, and

much did he admire one tall young stripling
who threw every opponent. At length, when
no man would stand up against him, the judges
awarded him the prize, which was a magnificent
horse with saddle and bridle all glittering with
gold.

Angry shouts arose when the decision was
made, and a number of bullies, with savage and
jealous cries of "Kill the stranger," rushed
upon the young man, who had perforce to fight
for his very life.

Quick as thought the knight and his men
entered the field and after a short, sharp scuffle
rescued the youth. Then, angrily turning in his
saddle, he addressed the seething mob:

"Shame on you, men of Mansfield. What if
the young man *be* a stranger? Did ye not allow
him to enter for the prize? And did he not
with excellent skill deserve it?"

" We be ashamed," answered a young wrestler,
stepping out from the crowd. "Right fairly did
he win the horse, and if he'll take my hand in
fellowship, here 'tis. I was champion of Mansfield afore this day dawned, but if any man
attempts further violence, let him deal with
me," he added, fiercely turning on his own
folk.

Seeing their own champion shake hands with

his conqueror, the townspeople were rightly
ashamed of their jealousy, and, led by Sir
Richard, they gave three ringing cheers for
the couple, and immediately all ill feeling
vanished as if by magic, and the merry fun
was resumed.

Some hours spent Sir Richard at the fair,
enjoying himself immensely, and then, calling
his men together, they resumed their broken
journey.

After riding for an hour or more the young
wrestler, mounted upon his prize, came galloping
up after them and asked leave to join their
party.

"For I have a cousin, one Robin Hood, an
outlaw, who lives in this forest, and I go to
seek him," said he.

"Then we are well met, young man," cried
Sir Richard joyfully. "For I go also to pay
your cousin a visit."

The afternoon was now far advanced, and at
a brisk pace the party rode on, blithely singing
thewhile. Dusk had fallen when they approached
the outlaws' headquarters, and Little John, who
was ever on the watch, rose up out of a mossy
dell to meet the intruders, whoever they might
be. His delight at seeing Sir Richard so richly
apparelled, and with such a splendid company

of followers, knew no bounds, and hurrying them all, they reached the glade.

Here Robin and good Friar Tuck were conversing together when John announced the guests; off fled the friar in hot haste, and immediately a fearful din of clattering pans and pots was heard.

Robin welcomed the long-expected arrival, whilst Sir Richard in a few words presented the bag of gold, explaining how he came by it, his tarrying at the wrestling match, and the rescue of a stranger, adding in conclusion: "The young man himself would speak with thee."

Then out stepped the tall youth, who had remained in the background till now. "Dost know me, Rob?" he asked.

"Will!" exclaimed Robin joyfully, and the two men embraced. "Good cousin," said Robin, after greetings had been exchanged, "what dost here?"

Then Will related how the old man his father had long been bullied by the steward in charge over the estate. How one day, on entering Gamwell Hall, he had been so enraged at the insults heaped upon his old father that he took the villain by the throat and flung him against the wall and broke his neck.

"He was a friend of Master Sheriff's, and the

Sheriff has sworn to have my life—so here I am.
Wilt thou have me, Robin?" he concluded
humbly.

"Gladly enough," laughed Robin, and then:
"It is many hours since we dined, and methinketh
by the goodly aroma Friar Tuck is ready for us.
Let's to our second feast!"

After the feast the good knight presented
Robin with the wonderful sword and the
splendid horse, and well pleased was he to own
such a blade and beast. Then Little John was
called, and with questioning wonder in his eyes
he rose up.

"Little John," said the knight, bowing, "thou
gavest a pair of spurs to a broken knight. Wilt
accept these in exchange?"

Still smiling, and amid further shouts of
delight, he stooped and fastened the handsome
spurs upon the heels of the grinning giant.

"Where is the good friar?" the knight asked
next, and renewed laughter went up as the
short, fat priest ran up, his jolly red face one
large smile of good nature, and a big white
apron, soiled with grease and dirt, covering a
good half of his little round body.

"Hail, thou king of priests and cooks!"
exclaimed Sir Richard, with grave humour.
"Thou gavest me thy helm, which I now wear,

and will ever wear. Do thou honour me by
wearing this cap," and diving into a large bag
at his side he displayed the glittering helmet.

Off came the friar's apron, and, proudly
donning the new cap, he thanked the knight,
saying: "Indeed I do thank you, Sir Knight
of the Sorrowful Face, but methinks you are
sad no more, therefore you shall be called 'Sir
Richard of the Smiling Countenance.'"

Even yet the knight had not bestowed all his
gifts, and now he produced the bows and quivers
and gave to each of Robin's outlaws, and soon
there was such a hubbub of excitement, for
every man stood possessed of the truest bow
that he had ever had.

Night had long since fallen, and Will Stutely,
who was ever for a joke, plucked Robin's sleeve
and reminded him that they had a new member
to their band and he had not yet been christened.

"Bring hither the friar and a bottle of wine,"
laughed Robin hilariously. "We'll soon remedy
that. What shall we call the babe?"

A loud hubbub ensued, till the friar raised
his hand for silence, and breaking off the neck
of the bottle poured the wine over poor Will's
red pate, saying in sepulchral tones:

"Will Gamwell of the red hair, henceforth
shalt thou be called Will Scarlet."

Long into the night did the revelry continue, and not until the first rays of dawn told of the coming of another day did they creep each to a chosen spot on the warm, soft turf, to be wrapt immediately in profound slumber.

Chapter XII

How Three Bold Archers Fought
Three Brave Foresters

ON a bright morning in midsummer Robin,
together with Little John and Will
Scarlet, set out in search of adventure.
They were weary of shooting deer, and all
wished that they could meet with sport more
worthy of their valour.

Accordingly, when they saw approaching
three King's foresters, they chuckled gleefully
and were right glad at the thought of a bout
with them. Tall men the strangers were, and
each was fully armed with sword and buckler,
together with a stout oak staff.

"Lo!" cried Robin in glee, "even according
to our wish have we met these likely fellows,
and before we part we'll prove their mettle!"
So saying, the three archers advanced boldly,
right happy in the thought of shrewd blows
and hard buffets.

The King's foresters presently came within a
few paces of the outlaws and halted suddenly.

"Robin Hood, as I am alive!" cried one of them in exultant tones.

"Himself," remarked Robin coolly and bowing low.

"Have at thee for a pestilent fellow," roared the keeper, enraged at the other's coolness. "Long have I prayed for this meeting, and now I have thee. Three of us to three of you. As for me—truly is my heart glad, for I have longed to meet thee in equal fight, and this day I am resolved to have a bout with thee."

"Beshrew me! but I like thee well," answered Robin. "With all my heart will I try a round with thee, and the contest shall determine whether King's foresters or outlaws be the better men."

The forthcoming combat was welcomed by the six excited men as they stripped, and where they threw their superfluous garments outlaw green and royal blue were seen to mingle.

At a given word they fell to, with eyes fierce with the lust of battle, and their staves smote heavily at each other for the space of two hours.

Now, to Robin's pride, the archers had proved superior, for the quarter-staff was the favourite weapon used by the King's foresters, and they had much vaunted their skill with it.

Robin had belaboured his man so well that he finally dropped his weapon and ruefully rubbed his head and then his sides.

Little John had knocked the staff from his adversary's hand by a well-directed blow and was now closing him round, whilst the other howled as he sought to escape the heavy blows.

Will Scarlet, who was not quite so skilful, was stooping over his opponent and feeling his head at the same time, and giving utterance to his thoughts: "The man could use his staff excellently well and has tanned my sore hide. However, I awaited my chance and——"

"Ugh!" came from the fallen man in tones of anguish. "How my poor head sings from that last blow. Never had I buffet like that before," and struggling painfully to his feet he staggered and would have fallen had not Will supported him and led him to the shade of a large overhanging tree.

"That was right warm work!" exclaimed Robin cheerfully, as the foresters begged leave for a breathing-space.

"Warm indeed!" snorted the chief forester, who lay panting on the greensward.

"Well, what think ye of Robin and of his friends, John and Will?" inquired Robin provokingly.

"Hard hitters i' faith," grudgingly admitted the forester. "But when we are refreshed, let us make trial and test whether you be as good at sword-play."

"Verily, I like thee more and more," chuckled Robin, pleased at such grudging praise from the King's own forester. "Immediately you are rested we'll satisfy you on that point."

Eager to regain their good name and perchance beat the outlaws, the rangers sprang up and declared they were ready, and drawing their swords the six men set upon one another in real good earnest. The archers were cool and sought to parry the blows, whilst the rangers beat heavily and tried to find a weak spot. So it was that unmercifully hard blows fell upon the bucklers of the outlaws and harmed them not.

For a long time Robin played thus with his foe, but at length he had the measure of his man, and as he pressed his point of vantage the other steadily gave ground before him.

Now that he had leisure to observe the movements of his men, Robin was dismayed to see that both were falling back before their opponents, a thing they had never been known to do before. So he pressed the harder upon his foe, so as to make him call out with fear.

Hearing the sound, the two rangers turned quickly, when Robin dropped the point of his sword to the ground and stood leaning on it. Then he gave vent to a loud laugh, and cried :

"Good lads all ! The best I have met. Surely 'twere pity to fight longer. Tell us your names, that ye may receive respect from us in the future."

John and Will Scarlet were mightily relieved at the interruption, whilst the two rangers flung themselves upon the earth, for they knew their leader was overmatched.

Right heartily did the foresters accept Robin's invitation to join them for further sport and refreshment, and soon a jovial company sat down to a generous meal in the greenwood.

Washing the meal down with first-rate wine, they afterward continued the contest, and again did the outlaws prove that though the King's men were passing good in their way, still the outlaws were always the victors.

Sworn brethren had they all become ere the afternoon was far advanced, and Robin said :

"At quarter-staff we be equal. At sword and buckler we are alike proficient. At the drinking-cup the outlaws can hold their own, but still we have the final test. Will you shoot with us ?"

"Aye!" roared the foresters, as in one voice.

"Good!" cried the outlaws, equally delighted.
"Shall we have a wager?" asked Robin, looking
at the rangers.

"Aye!" came the answer again. "All the
better!" declared the head forester.

"This shall be the wager," said Robin slowly.
"Should the King's rangers outshoot us, we will
do penance and become foresters of the King.
But should the King's rangers be beaten, then
will ye become outlaws and join Robin Hood's
band of merry men."

"Agreed!" roared the three, laughing, for
they were picked marksmen and were confident
they could beat any archer in the county.

Robin procured bows for them all, and a
suitable target was set up.

Will Scarlet and his comrade were the first.
The ranger, taking careful aim, planted his
arrow dead in the centre of the bull, whilst poor
Will, who was but a fair marksman, only scored
an inner.

Little John's adversary then took aim, but
being flushed with overmuch wine he was a
trifle careless, and his arrow alighted in the
outer circle.

Smilingly the tall giant shot, and his arrow
struck the mark by the side of the first ranger's.

The score was too nearly even to satisfy either party, and, realizing how much depended on his shot, the third ranger took careful and steady aim before he sped his shaft. But too careful was he, for he was allowing for a slight breeze, which, to his annoyance, dropped the moment the shaft went whizzing through the air. His arrow went an inch wide of the bull.

With a quiet smile playing round the corners of his mouth, Robin took his place and with a confident twang freed his arrow, which whistled off, and, quivering, split the first ranger's shaft in the centre of the bull.

With a very good grace the three foresters admitted their fair defeat and expressed their willingness to join Robin Hood's men.

The party now set off to join the rest of the outlaw band, who were surprised and delighted to see Robin, John, and Will, each arm in arm with a ranger in royal blue.

Chapter XIII

Robin is Beaten by a Beggar and Rescues the Widow's Three Sons

SOME weeks after the adventure with the King's foresters Robin purchased for himself a stout horse, and set off in high spirits to ride to Nottingham. Indeed, so gay and lively was he that he determined on a frolic.

Now it so happened that almost immediately he fell in with a poor beggar. A queer-looking fellow he was, too, with several bags hanging round his person, whilst his garments were split and torn past all recognition. The man himself was tall and strong and carried a stout club bound with iron.

Robin slowly cantered up to him. "A fine morning, friend!" quoth he. "Whither goest thou, and what countryman art thou?"

"A poor man from Yorkshire," returned the beggar. "Of your plenty, I beseech you, give me something!"

"Give *thee* something?" roared Robin, pre-

tending he was in a great rage. "A lusty
knave to beg on the King's highway! Be off,
or I'll put my sword about thy shoulders!"

"Touch me an thou dare," growled the beggar
in ominous tones. "Raise but a hand against
me and I'll smite thee from thy horse!"

Happy at the thought of a possible bickering,
Robin sprang down and hastily tore up a
sturdy ash plant. Immediately the beggar
faced about and stood on guard with his club.

Fiercely the two men grinned at each other,
and then the blows fell thick and fast.

Right well did the beggar defend himself;
but Robin was very sore, for the beggar's stick,
bound with iron, was a formidable weapon, and
in spite of all his efforts he could not get in
a blow with his sapling, and ever and again the
heavy cudgel came swinging against his ribs.
At last an extra hard blow on the crown
crushed all further desire for merriment out of
Robin Hood, and he wished he had let the
sturdy beggar proceed unmolested; for as the
outlaw grew weary the rogue seemed to gain
strength.

Presently the beggar seized his chance, and
with a deft side-stroke he smote the other on
his already bruised pate and sent him rolling in
the dust.

"Hold!" feebly cried he, as he staggered to his feet.

"That I will not," roared the beggar in high glee, "unless——" and he paused.

"Hand me thy horse and purse, and I'll let thee off!" he added impudently.

Robin pondered a moment, but, seeing no way out, he gave up his purse, exclaiming: "Better lose my belongings than my life!" and sighed as he reluctantly began to strip off his fine apparel. The beggar eagerly snatched these, and passed Robin filthy and evil-smelling rags to don.

Vastly pleased with his good luck, the beggar, now arrayed in Robin's finery, added a pair of spurs to his heels, buckled on his sword, and, vaulting into the saddle, threw the horn at the outlaw's head, and, with a great laugh, galloped off in fine style.

Full of groans and pains, Robin slowly made his way onward, and when but half an hour from Nottingham he met an old woman, who was moaning and sobbing and wringing her hands with grief.

Robin forgot his own troubles in the sight of the old woman's misery, and he gently approached, saying kindly:

"Don't cry so, mother, but tell a poor beggar thy grief and he'll help if he can!"

In a voice broken by great sobs the old dame told him her sad story.

She was a widow with three stalwart sons, and they all lived in a small hut on the verge of the forest. Often her sons had shot and brought home one of the King's deer, and, because money was so scarce with them, it had provided good food for some days; but that very morning they had been caught red-handed by the Sheriff's men and were taken captives to Nottingham.

"The Sheriff is a hard man," wailed the wretched mother; "and to-day at sunset they are to be hanged!" After the fresh outburst of sobbing had subsided a little she told the beggar she was on her way to the forest to find Robin Hood and ask his help.

Robin at once revealed himself, and, excusing his dirty rags, he comforted the woman and told her to go home and that he would save her three sons. Having seen her drooping figure totter out of sight, his first thought was for a messenger, and, forgiving the beggar for flinging his horn at him, he wound a long blast upon it, and very shortly an archer emerged from out of the shrubbery near by.

"Haste to Little John!" cried Robin. "Tell him to bring a hundred men to the

ROBIN HOOD AND THE POOR WIDOW

market-place one hour before sunset this day. All must be disguised differently, so as to mingle in the crowd. Every one must have sword and buckler concealed about his person and must be ready when I signal. Describe my dress to Little John!"

The messenger set off at high speed, whilst Robin turned once more toward Nottingham town. On entering the gates he was greeted familiarly by the keeper.

"Ha! ha! friend Giles," quoth that cheery knave, "thou art just in time again. There be three lusty youths to hang this day."

Now did Robin heartily rejoice in his heart that he had met the beggar, for it was in truth Giles the hangman that had made off with his clothes, money, and horse. Nevertheless, he determined to play hangman that day, and somehow save those three sons of the widow.

Many a clod of earth struck Robin as he proceeded along the road, and, losing his temper at last, he turned and shook his club threateningly at the mob. A stone whizzing past his ear confirmed the idea that friend Giles was well hated, and so, gathering his tattered clothes firmly about him, Robin ran, and sped toward the prison gates. He was full of wrath and indignation, and his face was spattered with mud, when he reached the prison, where he was taken before the Sheriff.

"Glad indeed am I to see thee, Giles!" declared that pompous personage. For well did he remember the time when Giles was absent and Robin Hood had taken the hangman's place. Yet even now he could not look upon a ditch without shuddering. So he greeted Giles like an old friend.

"Have no fear, your worship," growled Giles sulkily. "After the treatment I've suffered to-day at their hands—I'll make them suffer. There'll be no hitch to-day."

For Robin was so bespattered with mud that his features were concealed, and no one guessed that he was not the real Giles.

One hour before the time appointed the cart was brought round, and in it stood the three prisoners and a priest, and the hangman was told to get in also.

Carefully guarded by a strong force of the Sheriff's men, the sad procession wound its way heavily through the main streets and so into the market-place.

A gibbet had been erected, and stood out darkly against the rays of the declining sun, whilst three ropes swung gently to and fro in the evening breeze.

The priest having concluded his ministrations, Giles and the three prisoners were helped upon the platform, where he had to tie the hands of the condemned men, the while earnestly peering at the faces in the crowd.

Very thankful was he to spy Little John and Will Scarlet, and far away he saw Will Stutely and many more of his men, yet so well were they scattered amongst the multitude that none save he could have picked them out. Then he loosely placed the noose of rope round each young neck, and those nearest saw the young men straighten up and their faces clear as if some mysterious influence was at work which bade them take fresh courage.

All was ready, and the hangman stood awaiting the Sheriff's word. A moment or two, amidst intense stillness, and the great ball of liquid fire sank beyond the horizon. The Sheriff raised his hand.

A great groan arose from the people, and most of them turned their heads away and shuddered violently. Those who were hardened, however, still kept their eyes riveted on the gallows, and presently a cry of relief and joy went ringing up, as the hangman, instead of hauling up the rope, pulled out a horn from beneath his tunic and blew a short, sharp blast.

Now was every eye fixed upon the platform in spellbound fascination, as a hundred determined archers forced their way to the front.

The Sheriff's chief officer bravely sprang upon the steps to seize the hangman, but Robin smote him with his iron-bound staff, so that he fell and lay back as dead.

Now did the outlaws rally round Robin and the three youths, and so fiercely did they fight that soon they had the mastery over the Sheriff's men. Then, before the garrison could be fetched, the party of outlaws, with the condemned men and the hangman at their head, had triumphantly left the city.

Great was the widow's joy as she beheld her lads again, and over and over again did she thank Robin, and with many tears did she bless him. Night having fallen, and the widow dreading a reprisal, the outlaws camped round the hut that night, and early next morning they removed the old dame and her home to their own camp, where the sons took up service with Robin Hood, and the old woman waited upon the young wife of Allan-a-Dale.

Chapter XIV

Maid Marian

THERE had been great sports at Finsbury Fields, and King Henry was in high glee, for his picked team of ten archers had shot well and truly, and had carried off all the chief prizes.

"Fine men, all of them," said he to the Queen, as they were discussing the merits of the various competitors, and then he went on:

"Friends Tepus, Clifton, and Gilbert are the three finest archers in the whole country."

"Enough of these men!" returned the Queen tartly. "I am weary of hearing their praises!" Then after a slight pause she added: "I will wager I can find three who will outshoot them. Yea, and by St Bartholomew's Day."

Eagerly the King accepted the challenge and caused great preparation to be made for a festival on the forthcoming saint's day.

Now it wanted some twenty days before the feast of St Bartholomew, and the Queen was sore perplexed as to where she might find her vaunted champions. In her difficulty one of her waiting-maids approached her. She was the lovely daughter of Robert, Earl of Huntingdon, and was called Marian.

Said she to the Queen: "May it please your Grace, I know a man who would proudly shoot for you. I speak of Robin Hood of Sherwood Forest."

The Queen listened with interest, and, drawing the blushing maiden to a stool at her feet, encouraged her with questions, until she had confessed that she knew Robin Hood, the notorious outlaw. The Queen looked startled for a moment, but then, with a kindly gesture, she put a protecting arm round the girl's shoulders, whilst Marian related, with glowing cheeks and starlit eyes, how her cousin, having broken the neck of his father's impudent steward, had fled to the greenwood, and there sought out his kinsman, Robin Hood, and joined his band of outlaws. But she did not tell how in former happier days, when Robin was a free man, they had exchanged vows of love and sworn to be true to one another. Neither did she mention who gave her the golden arrow that she wore pinned to her bodice. But many other matters concerning Robin Hood she related with enthusiasm, until the Queen was impressed by the skill and boldness of his exploits, and longed to see the man.

Marian told her that Robin himself was a most gentle and kind man, and the Queen, knowing by hearsay that they were marvellous bowmen, determined to ask his help at the contest.

Then there arose the question of a messenger, when, with a pretty blush, Marian offered to go; and amidst much laughter and friendly raillery the Queen and Marian retired to a private chamber, where they discussed the best way of reaching the outlaw's retreat in safety.

Next morning a handsome youth, riding a splendid horse, rode slowly out of the courtyard of the palace, attended by a good company of troopers, and none save the Queen knew who he was, and the nature of his errand. Merrily they cantered, revelling in the pure country air and the very joy of living. At length they arrived in Nottingham town without mishap, where they rested for the night. Early next morning the youth set off on foot, and alone, and within a short time was treading the grassy glades of Sherwood.

Now this self-same morning found Robin doleful and sad, for one of his gloomy fits was

upon him. Refusing all offers of companion-
ship, he set off, bow in hand, moodily reflecting
on the former days of happiness he had spent
as a free citizen.

Poor Robin was too proud to confide his
secret even to Little John, and so when his
heart yearned for his love he would stride off
into the deepest dells and would be lost to the
camp for days at a stretch, until his good
humour returned. At such a time his men
would look at him with awe and dare scarcely
open their lips to speak, whilst Little John
gazed sadly at his master and wondered at the
cause.

This morning, however, he was not to be left
in peace, for even as he sat down in the very
heart of the forest a herd of deer fled swiftly
by. Angry at being disturbed, and wrathful
that anyone should dare hunt without his
permission in these unfrequented spots, Robin
rose hastily, with a fierce expression that boded
no good to the trespasser. An arrow whistled
past his head, and he saw the leader of the herd
jump high in the air and then fall to earth.
Turning to see whence the arrow came, Robin
saw a gay youth, richly apparelled, running
gleefully toward the fallen buck. Robin
straightway started up and cried:

"Ho, stripling! and who art thou that makest so free with the King's deer?"

"Away, fellow!" commanded the youth. "My name, forsooth? An thou givest me any more of thine impudence I'll carve it on thy back!"

Robin, speechless with rage, drew his sword, and the stripling being no whit afraid, they were quickly cutting and parrying at each other.

After a short time Robin's good nature returned, and the valiant nature of the slender youth in standing up to fight so tickled his fancy that as they fought he smiled.

Now the youth, seeing that smile, became suddenly enraged and tried to rain harder blows. Robin merely smiled more broadly, and the stripling, finding he could not penetrate the smiling man's guard, almost wept with rage and vexation.

Having reduced the young man to the point of desperation, Robin made a feint and slipped. With a joyous shout the youth lunged forward and wounded him in the wrist.

Robin at once threw away his sword and begged for mercy, which the young man granted with much condescension.

"And now, fellow," said he, "I seek Robin

Hood! Knowst thou anything of him, and where I may find him?"

"Yea," answered Robin meekly. "I am of his band and will lead you to him."

But Robin was sore puzzled as to where he had heard that voice before, so he asked a question:

"I prithee, stranger, who are you?"

"I am Richard Partington, a page at the Court of my lady the Queen, and I carry an important message to thy master."

He then noticed that the wounded wrist was still bleeding and cried in alarm:

"Good fellow, I have hurt thee. Prithee, let me bind thy wrist."

And Robin still puzzled his brain over the familiar voice, yet he mechanically held out his arm. The stripling proceeded to take out a dainty cambric handkerchief from his bosom and wrapt it round the wrist. Giving it an extra tightening before he made the knot caused the wound to twinge and made Robin glance down quickly. His eye fell upon the white fingers of the youth, and upon one of them glittered and sparkled the very ring he had given to his love long ago.

He jerked his hand away and took hold of those slender wrists with masterful force, and they gazed into the depths of each other's eyes, when Robin broke the spell by crying joyfully: "Surely I do know thee now. Thou art Marian!"

"Robin!"

With a great sob of joy, he embraced her, and much sweet talk had they together.

Marian was greatly distressed that she had not known her lover at first.

"Nay, but the forest life changeth a man!" exclaimed Robin cheerfully, and then roguishly putting her from him for a moment he continued:

"And thou, good mistress, surely I knew thee not. Yet in future shall I be afraid of all pages."

And Robin, perceiving she was ashamed, took off his cloak and wrapped her in it.

"The wound," said he, laughing, "is but the merest scratch. But I shall ever cherish the scar."

Happily they took their way to the camp, and for once Robin did not try a short cut. As they slowly sauntered, Marian explained that as a Queen's messenger she had come dressed as a page and gave the Queen's invitation.

Robin's eyes sparkled, and he joyously accepted. By this time they had reached the

ROBIN HOOD AND MAID MARIAN

outlaws' retreat, and as Robin blew a loud blast upon his horn the whole band assembled.

Will Scarlet at once recognized the sweet face beneath the drooping plumes, and, jumping forward, he took her in both arms and kissed her heartily upon both cheeks. Then, whispering aside with Robin, he turned round to the band and announced, with a very important air :

"Merry men all! to-day the band welcomes its mistress. Maid Marian, who is to wed our master, Robin Hood!"

Amid deafening cheers from the delighted outlaws the blushing and happy Marian was given into the tender care of the sweet wife of Allan-a-Dale, and later in the evening, attired once more in bodice and kirtle, and looking more winsome than ever, she took her seat at Robin's right hand at a great feast of welcome, at which every outlaw was present.

Early next morning Robin and Marian, who were loath to leave the beautiful greenwood, together with Allan-a-Dale and his wife, and the pick of the most skilful archers, set out on their way to London town.

Chapter XV

The King's Archery Contest at Finsbury Field

APARTMENTS for Robin and his men were found within the palace itself, yet so well was the secret kept that no man knew of the Queen's guests.

Greatly pleased to find Robin Hood no rough forest dweller, but a courtly gentleman, the Queen promised to speak to the King on his behalf.

Will Scarlet was no stranger to her Majesty. Indeed before he was outlawed he had been a great favourite at Court.

A merry company now met in the Queen's private chamber, and there in the evenings Allan-a-Dale would delight her Majesty, for right cunningly did he play upon his harp and sweetly did he sing of the outlaws' merry deeds in the greenwood. Sometimes Little John and Will Stutely would give an exhibition of quarter-staff, and what with amusement at the great height of the giant and the shortness and stoutness of Will, and admiration of their great skill, never had the Queen and her ladies been so entertained.

The Queen took a great liking to all the outlaws, and she was never weary of hearing from Robin or Will Scarlet stories of their exploits, and the one she liked best of all was that one which told how my lord the Bishop of Hereford dined with Robin.

Pleasantly the days passed, and the morning of St Bartholomew dawned fair and bright.

Before the sun peeped over the housetops the Queen summoned Robin before her.

"Good Robin," said she, in gracious tones, "even now the King has gone over to Finsbury. Do thou therefore prepare thine archers and repair to the field. Presently I will be there, and as soon as may be I will cause a horn to be blown. Then do thou and thy men step forth and stand before the King."

Immediately Robin withdrew from the royal presence, and having given orders for all his men to be clothed in Lincoln green, with large hats in which waved a white feather, he dressed himself in scarlet from head to foot. Soon all were ready, and, making their way to the scene of the contest, were safely hidden on the outskirts of the field.

Whilst the common people waited and discussed the chances of their favourite archers, the lords and ladies slowly strolled into the grounds and took their seats, and soon after the blare of trumpets announced the approach of their Majesties.

Amid much cheering and stamping of feet the royal pair took their places; and when all was quiet once more the King called his bowman Tepus and bade him measure the distance, so that he might know how far the mark was.

A long range was marked out by the archer, and then he returned to the King.

"Sire," he cried, and bowed low, "I have measured a good bowman's range—full fifteen score yards is the distance from the mark to the target."

"Good, worthy Tepus," returned the King. Turning to the Queen, he laughed merrily. " A goodly range, my lady, and one which will try thy champions! And now, let us see! For what wager shall we shoot?"

> "Three hundred tuns of Rhenish wine,
> Three hundred casks of beer, and
> Three hundred of the fattest bucks that run."

called out the Queen, as if she had had the wager long since settled.

The King made a grimace. "In good sooth, that is indeed a princely wager! Yet cheerfully do I accept! Do thou therefore bring forth thine archers, that the shooting may begin."

The Queen beckoned to a page, and he sounded his horn. In a moment Robin Hood, Will Stutely, and Little John stood face to face with their King. Much relieved was the Queen to see that no man knew them.

"Come hither!" she cried to Sir Richard of the Lea, who stood near by the royal box. "Surely thou art of ancient lineage and honourable. Wilt thou lay a wager with me?"

He gave one keen glance at the three Queen's champions that penetrated all disguise, then he answered: "Nay, gracious lady, I am unwilling to wager against my Queen, for in my heart I hope for your success."

With an engaging smile the Queen turned to the Bishop of Hereford, saying:

"Surely your Grace will wager with me? Or perhaps you would prefer to wager on my men?"

"By my mitre," declared the Bishop bluntly, "I would not bet a single penny against the King's archers!"

"How much will you bet on them?" interposed Robin quietly.

"All the money in my purse will I wager against thee and thine!" cried the Bishop.

"What is in your purse?" asked Robin calmly.

"Fifteen score nobles," answered the other. "Nigh on a hundred pounds!"

"Throw your purse on the ground!" exclaimed Robin, and taking his own bag of money from his belt he threw it with the other.

The archers now took their places at the mark, and boastful Clifton exclaimed:

"I'll lay my bow I'll pierce the centre every time!"

With that the King's men shot, and each man found the bull's-eye, while Robin and his men purposely missed the target.

The Queen looked very downcast, whilst the Bishop turned his eyes gloatingly upon the two purses.

The target was removed and a willow wand set up, and again the archers shot. This time the King's men missed the mark entirely, but Robin split the wand and the others each grazed it, and so scored a hit.

Now did the Queen smile right happily, but the Bishop looked glum and morose.

This made the score equal.

"Three each!" cried the King. "The next three pays for all."

Clifton took careful aim, but his arrow whizzed within an inch of the wand. Will Stutely shot next, and his arrow shaved the mark.

One to the Queen's men.

Gilbert took his place, and shot a better shaft than ever he did before, for his arrow split the wand in two.

A new wand was set up, and Little John, knowing he could not beat this shot, tried his best to equal it.

A sigh escaped the Queen, and her ladies looked startled, as the arrow whizzed past the mark and buried itself in the ground beyond.

Much downcast, the giant stepped aside, and the score was now even. Excitement prevailed everywhere. The deciding shots were to be made: Tepus, the King's own bow-bearer and the best shot in London, against Robin Hood the outlaw.

Very carefully did Tepus loose his shaft. But it struck the side of the wand and then sped on.

Robin rejoiced to see the wand still uncloven, and, fitting his arrow, he calmly took a steady aim. He released the shaft; with a twang it sped swiftly onward and cleft the wand from top to bottom.

Merrily laughed the Queen, and very unhappy looked the Bishop as Will Scarlet picked up the purses and handed them to Robin.

Shouts and exclamations, mingling with grumblings and altercations, rose on all sides, for all had thought the King's archers could not be beaten.

"Thou hast fairly won," declared the King to his Queen. "Never saw I such shooting before!"

At these words the Queen swept him a profound curtsy, as she meekly murmured : "Sire, I crave a boon."

"Whatever thou wishest is granted willingly," answered the King lightly.

"I beg that thou wilt not be angry with any of my champions," she returned entreatingly.

"Who could be angry with such excellent bowmen ?" exclaimed her lord, with amazement.

Then turning, the Queen cried out gleefully : "Ye are pardoned, Robin Hood and Little John, Will Stutely, Will Scarlet, and all of ye."

When the King had found voice he exclaimed feebly : "Is this Robin Hood, and are these his men ? Surely, I had thought him dead and his band long since dispersed," and he frowned ever so slightly.

The rueful Bishop said sadly : "Had I known it was *that* bold outlaw I had not wagered a single penny." Then turning to the King he added : "May it please your Grace, this fellow took me prisoner one Saturday and bound me fast to a tree, and made me sing Mass for himself and his villains. Then he robbed me of five hundred pounds and tied me backward upon my horse, and so sent me on my way," he ended in an aggrieved tone.

"And what if I did?" asked Robin boldly. "Right glad was I to see you, for I had not heard Mass for full six months."

What the Queen whispered to the King we know not, but his frown melted into a smile, and the smile broke out into a laugh.

"Welcome, bold Robin!" he cried. "Full forty days mayest thou abide in this town, but after that thou must depart again."

With much feasting and revelry the forty days too soon came to an end, and Robin, after fondly bidding his love farewell, bade the Queen adieu, and with his men took the road north that would finally bring them home to Sherwood once again.

Chapter XVI

King Richard Visits Sherwood Forest

SOON after the events recorded in the preceding chapter King Henry the Second died and his son King Richard sat upon the throne. Robin hoped now to be released from outlawry, but Richard set out for the Holy Land, and so for some years matters went on as before. At last, owing to a determined attempt by the royal forces to suppress the Sherwood outlaws, Robin Hood deemed it wise to disband his followers for a year. He himself spent most of the time near the Yorkshire coast, where his name is still associated with a picturesque fishing hamlet, perched upon the sides of a rugged ravine, that opens on a tiny bay a few miles south of Whitby.

Hearing of the return of Richard I from the Crusades, Robin thought that the time was favourable for the old life in the forest to be resumed. So he joyfully set out over the moors for the beloved glades of Sherwood.

One evening, just as the sun was setting,

weary and footsore, he reached the borders of
the forest. Another hour of steady trudging
brought him right into the very glade which
had once been a joyous and merry camp. His
keen eye took in all details of the glade, and he
noted at once the signs of human habitation.
A cloak lay under a spreading oak-tree, proving
that the owner was not very far away, whilst
the embers of a dying fire still glowed red.

Robin was surprised, but after a moment's
consideration he placed his horn to his lips
and blew thereon a clear blast. He listened to
the echoes repeating again and again this long
familiar call, until, just as the last echo could be
heard like a hushed whisper, a clump of trees
parted and there stood a huge form. The giant
at once gave a great whoop of joy and came
running full speed to within a yard of Robin.

"Welcome back, my master! Welcome back,
good Robin!"

"Ha! Ha! Little John, my friend," cried
Robin, in great glee, "glad am I to meet
thee!"

We may be quite sure that they spent a very
happy evening together, and indeed it was
almost dawn before they thought of sleep.

Robin awoke early next morning, to find the
sun right overhead, and laughingly chid himself

for a sluggard, and then looked round for Little John, but the giant was not to be seen. So he whiled away an hour or so tending his bow and testing his skill.

Now very early Little John had arisen and hastened away to Friar Tuck, who had retired into a hermit's cave since the band had dispersed.

"Robin has returned!" he announced in tones of suppressed excitement to the jovial friar.

"Say you so, John?" calmly returned the other. "I knew he would come back soon."

The friar unearthed his bow and arrows from their hiding-place and prepared to depart.

Happy as larks, the two men strode through the forest glades. On the way they shot a fine buck, and they entered the secret glade just as Robin was about to leave it in search of Little John.

Very joyfully did the worthy friar greet Robin, and Robin was no whit less pleased to see him. Then he hastened away to his old pantry, and with improvised cooking utensils he soon had savoury portions of venison roasting before a glowing fire. The smell soon drew Robin and Little John, and as the three sat round and enjoyed the meal many a tale of brave doing did Little John tell, and Friar Tuck had much to say of the hospitality of strangers, whilst Robin recounted his adventures in Yorkshire.

Late in the afternoon Will Scarlet, arm in arm with Will Stutely, entered the glade, and seeing the three figures round the fire, ran forward and welcomed Robin, and were welcomed by the others.

Next morning Robin sent his two lieutenants in search of the merry men, and all that day and the day following they spread the news of Robin's return in the hamlets and villages around.

By twos and threes the archers returned to the camp, and at the end of the first week they came back in little companies, and wholeheartedly took up service again under their beloved leader. By the end of the month the band had reached its full number and once again the welkin rang with the noise of horn and merry laughter.

With light hearts they returned to their old life, in which, whilst levying illegal toll from the wealthy, they generously assisted and befriended the poor and oppressed. Many a rich wayfarer and many a portly prelate entered the forest blithely and left it a sadder and a poorer man. Yet many a poor man blessed Robin for food and money given, when driven to desperate straits. With women his men were especially gentle.

Before long the exploits of Robin Hood and his merry men reached the ears of the newly returned King. He had been absent from his kingdom for five years, so that he had not before heard of the outlaw until tidings reached him of these daring robberies of priests and nobles. Then he determined to put an end to such lawless deeds. It must be confessed, however, that the King secretly admired the fearlessness and courage of Robin Hood. He was told by one of his advisers how the party that went to bring him captive had returned empty-handed, not having so much as seen a single archer, because the band had for the time dispersed. "Indeed, my liege," said the wise old man, "I ween the only way to see Robin Hood is to go disguised as a wealthy abbot."

A merry laugh was the only reply to this shrewd advice.

Some few days later Robin received word that his old friend, Sir Richard of the Lea, purposed paying him a visit. Now Robin dearly loved the good knight, and on the morning when Sir Richard was due he caused a great feast to be prepared, and together with

Little John and Will Scarlet took the road, intending to meet their honoured guest.

Hardly had they travelled a mile when they spied a company on horseback trotting along toward them. Five monks there were, and a leader — a strongly built man clad in a russet gown, the hood of which completely covered his head, only his piercing eyes glittering in the shadow. He rode a magnificent black horse.

"More guests!" observed Robin, with a twinkle in his eyes.

Then Little John said : " Methinks yon black charger is the very one thou hast so often longed for."

Out stepped bold Robin, as he seized the leader's bridle.

"Give thee greeting, Sir Priest," he said pleasantly. "Wilt thou and thy company honour our festive board this day?"

"King's messengers are we, therefore allow us to pass on our way," replied the big leader, with dignity.

"If ye be the King's messengers, then surely must ye dine with me. Then, having been refreshed, ye shall have two men to speed you on your way, for I am a true King's man," answered Robin.

"We thank thee for thy hospitality," said the tall man. "Lead on quickly, for our errand is urgent and brooks not delay."

Just then Sir Richard and his company were observed at the crest of the wood, so Robin and the King's messengers were constrained to wait for a few minutes till the others came up. Robin and Sir Richard hugely entertained the burly stranger, who rode between them, with jokes and stories, and more than once his laugh rang out loudly.

Right royal was the feast prepared by the jolly friar, and half a dozen stalwart archers waited immediately upon the needs of Sir Richard and their new guest, and plied them with meat and drink with courteous hospitality.

"Sir Priest," said Robin, "can ye not stay to watch our forest sports, or must ye pursue your journey immediately?" For Robin Hood was justly proud of the skill of his band of outlaws, and seized every opportunity of showing off their prowess to strangers.

"Art thou not Robin Hood?" demanded he of the russet gown, with startling directness.

"Yea," answered Robin, nothing abashed.

"I thought so," said the other; "for tales of thy dinners have reached even unto my humble monastery. And now my journey is ended. Know this, Robin Hood, King Richard of England demands thy presence in London town within seven days, there to account for thy deeds and misdeeds. A fair trial shalt thou have, to which purpose here is the royal summons."

"Sir Priest," answered Robin proudly, "go tell the King that Robin Hood is his faithful liege and servant ; that within seven days he and his men will stand before him and submit to his will." And then he added, almost anxiously : "And now, your quest ended, ye will stay our honoured guests and watch our forest sports, that you may take back word unto King Richard."

"Willingly," responded the priest.

Then commenced the merry greenwood games, with quarter-staff bouts, jumping, wrestling, fencing, shooting, and other exercises of manly strength wherein the men delighted. Last of all came the shooting match. The rules of this contest provided that every archer should shoot at a given mark, but he who missed should receive a buffet from the brawny arm of fat Friar Tuck.

One or two archers who missed ruefully walked up to the friar, who, after a word or two of rebuke or, perchance, consolation if it was a particularly good archer, would then deal the unfortunate man a blow that never failed to floor him.

Little John had the misfortune to miss the target, and many were the shouts as he too toppled and fell before the huge fist of the valiant friar. Now, whether Robin was wilfully careless or had not recovered after laughing over the giant's discomfiture matters not, but when his turn came to shoot he also missed.

With pretended humility he stepped up to receive his buffet, and this time Little John's large guffaw was heard above all the laughter.

But Robin was wily, and turning to the King's messenger he said:

"Good Sir Priest, I desire that thou, our honoured guest, deal me my stroke!"

"Not so!" roared the fat friar. "'Tis for me to deal the buffet!"

"Nay, good Robin," replied the priest in solemn tones, "let the friar deal the blow. Though, were it not for my priestly office, I would gladly smite thee, friendly!"

Taking the words for an insult to himself, Friar Tuck fired up in an instant.

"Am I not a priest? There is no disgrace in being both man and priest! I would thou couldst forget thy dignity and have a buffet with me, and the better man of us twain could deal Robin his blow."

The challenge was received with cheers from all the band, and the King's messenger had perforce to acquiesce. He stepped up, a fine figure of a man, too fine a man to be clothed in the protecting garb of a monk, and bared his arm, as tough and knotty an arm as you could find anywhere.

"Verily, thou art a priest after my own heart. For the honour of my monastery I'll buffet thee. Do thou take thy blow first," he added graciously.

Back stepped the friar, who fully intended the other should not have a chance to deal his blow, and with a terrific thud the heavy fist fell full upon the chest of the priest, who staggered a little but kept his feet.

"A shrewd blow and a strong," he remarked casually. "Now stand ye for mine!" Out shot his fist and the friar toppled clean over and lay gasping on his back.

The force of the blow, however, had caused the priest's hood to fall back, and his head and features, which had hitherto been concealed, were now revealed in the broad light of day. Crisp, fair curls clustered over his forehead instead of the usual shaven crown. Sir Richard, who had often been to Court, and Will Scarlet, who had served under the late King, at once recognized the handsome and bold features of Richard Cœur de Lion and with a cry of "The King!" they fell on one knee before him.

All was confusion for a moment, till Robin also bent his knee, and the rest of the band followed suit.

"Sire," Robin pleaded humbly, "I crave your pardon for myself and all these, my men. We have ever been your Majesty's faithful servants, and have but resisted the oppression of unfaithful servants of the crown. Your deer we have slain—abbots we have relieved of their oft ill-gotten riches. Yet have we befriended the poor and aided the widow and fatherless."

The simple confession ended, Robin and all his company knelt with heads bared and bowed, waiting for the judgment of their King.

"Rise, good Robin!" cried the King genially. "I forgive thee and all thy men. What boots it that ye have eased a few rich abbots? Methinks I myself have also eased some, and I shall certainly relieve more, for I have heard of their oppression of the poor. Yet though we freely forgive thee, one thing I command—that ye all take service under me as my bodyguard.

Thou, Robin, shalt still be captain, with Little John as thy lieutenant. Now what say ye? Will ye be my archers?"

A lusty shout went forth from every throat in answer.

A week later, amid great rejoicing, King Richard, escorted by his new bodyguard, reached London town. We may be quite sure that Maid Marian was among the first to greet the honoured captain of the guard.

Chapter XVII

The Marriage and Death of Robin Hood

GREAT was the stir and bustle in London town one brilliant day in May, for Robin Hood, captain of the King's archers, and the King's right-hand man, was to be married to the lovely daughter of the Earl of Huntingdon.

Great throngs of people of all classes pressed into the church, for the bride was to be given away by the King himself.

At length, at the appointed time, Robin, escorted by Will Scarlet, now no less a personage than Sir William Gamwell of Gamwell Hall, and Little John, now Head Forester of Sherwood, entered the church and took up their places at the altar rails.

A great roar of cheering announced the near approach of the bride.

The Archbishop, robed in rich vestments, officiated, and a burly priest, no less a man than good Friar Tuck himself, assisted with dignity at the ceremony.

149

The marriage service proceeded solemnly, without any untoward event, and at the close King Richard heartily kissed the lovely bride and wished the happy pair every joy.

Robin Hood, with his beautiful wife upon his arm, left the church a proud and happy man.

As they passed along the streets they were greeted with loud cheers by the people, who thronged to see the hero of Sherwood Forest.

For some months after their marriage Robin was blissfully happy and took delight in his new duties as captain of the King's bodyguard, but alas! Marian developed symptoms of an incurable disease, and in alarm Robin begged the royal permission to retire from the Court.

The King showed his sympathy by allowing them both to retire at once.

Now Sir Richard of the Lea lived in a castle upon a hill overlooking Nottingham, and Robin had an idea that if Marian lived there awhile the strong, pure air might cure her, so after a long and weary journey they reached the town, where they were met by Sir Richard and his lady.

Sorely grieved were they to see Marian looking so pale and wan, and with the utmost tenderness they bore her to the castle.

Nevertheless, in spite of all the loving care

and attention of Robin and his hostess, poor Marian drooped and faded from day to day. Soon it was apparent even to her husband that she would never recover.

One evening, Sir Richard and his wife being out of the room, poor Robin, almost heartbroken with grief, was gazing sadly at his wife as she lay in a light sleep. Suddenly her eyes opened, and with a touch of her old gay spirit she cried : "Good Queen, I'll find an archer who'll overshoot all the King's men!" Even as she finished speaking the fire in her eyes died down, and she looked at Robin and knew him. A lovely smile of perfect peace stole over her wasted features, and whispering feebly, "Robin, my own love," her eyes closed, and her pure spirit fled.

*　　　*　　　*　　　*　　　*

After Marian's death Robin was inconsolable, and the King, pitying him intensely, sent him on a mission to foreign lands.

The change of scene softened Robin's anguish, and some three years later he returned to England ; but no longer was he the merry-hearted Robin ; yet to all who required sympathy he was ever gentle and tender-hearted.

But his peaceful life was not destined to be of long duration, for King John had in the meantime succeeded his brother Richard, and he made no attempt to disguise his ill will toward Robin, and his distrust of the archers of the bodyguard.

One day he insulted Robin past all endurance, who with a flash of his old spirit returned a hot answer.

"Treason!" roared the King, and in a very short time Robin was made a prisoner and confined to the Tower.

Will Stutely and several other bold archers who could not bear to think of their loved leader pining in prison made plans for his escape. So one night the watchmen were overpowered and Robin was released. Three days later Robin took up his old quarters in Sherwood Forest.

Week followed week, but never did one pass in which one or another of the old members did not find his way back to the camp, for to one and all the call of the wild woods kept ringing in their ears and they could not stay away.

But one fair summer's day the outlaws were disporting themselves at their manly games of skill when an alarm was raised.

Silently each man sprang to his arms and prepared for a fight. A great tramping of feet was heard through the crackling brushwood and some forty of the King's foresters, led by the giant Little John, entered the camp.

"How now, Friend John?" cried Robin sharply. "Art come to lead us to Nottingham Jail?"

"Nay!" came in a roar from the old familiar voice. "Art in need of a lieutenant and some goodly men?" Overjoyed was Robin, for Little John had ever a warm corner in his heart.

Then Little John burst out with his news:

"This morning," he said, with a merry laugh, "I received his gracious Majesty's command to hand over my authority to a worthier keeper. With my authority I handed over my staff, and the 'worthier man,' having a somewhat tender pate, will not be able to commence his duties for some weeks. These men have refused to serve under such a weakling and so I ventured to invite them to come with me. Stout men they be and excellent with a good oak staff."

Robin cast an eye approvingly over the stalwart new-comers and without more ado enrolled them in his band.

King John proved a bitter enemy, however, and sent company after company to harass the outlaws.

The band was never safe now—even the new

King's foresters sought them out to slay them, and the men were continually called upon to arm and defend themselves. Each time, however, a few brave archers fought their last fight, and some of the more timid began to desert. Some fled to Derbyshire and some to Yorkshire, and the outlaw band dwindled down to some three score men.

Whilst it was in this low state word came from Nottingham that a company of five hundred veteran soldiers was marching on Sherwood. Rallying his men for a final stand, Robin determined to show a bold front, and he hoped by personal valour to inspire his men to victory.

But it was not to be. Fighting hard, the band was driven from its stronghold and was split up into several small companies. Though stubbornly contesting every inch, the soldiers gradually drove them out of the forest. Robin and Little John had kept together, and at last, seeing that all was indeed over, Robin for the last time blew the old and stirring blast.

It was the end. Hearing the familiar call, his wearied men knew that Robin had given up hope and the day was lost. Some surrendered, whilst those who were able fled.

Robin and Little John hastened away to the North. Their progress was hindered by a troublesome wound that Robin had received, which, though it did not appear serious, would not heal.

On the fifth day of their flight he could go no farther, for a fever had settled upon him.

"Lead my horse," said he to his companion, "and carry me to Kirklees Abbey. Once I rendered a small service to the Abbess there and maybe she will give us shelter."

All that day Little John rode silently on, and late in the afternoon they arrived at the nunnery, tired and hungry. Loudly the giant hammered at the gates and called for hospitality for a sick man. After a long interval the Abbess, a tall, white-faced woman, allowed the travellers to enter. At her request Little John carried the sick man to a chamber, where he laid him gently down, and then left him to the tender care of the nuns.

The wounded man then confessed to the Abbess that he was indeed that bold outlaw Robin Hood, but that he had a grievous wound and was in dire need of rest. "I pray thee," he concluded weakly, "send for a leech that he may bleed me, that soon I may pursue my way."

Smoothing the fevered brow with her cool fingers, she told Robin that she had great skill with healing herbs and would herself gently bleed away the poisoned blood and with sweet oils quickly heal him.

Content, Robin sank back upon his couch and, being greatly fatigued, fell into a deep slumber.

Now, whether the pale Abbess hoped for great reward, we know not, but, whatever her motive, a cruel and treacherous act was hers.

Without a glance at the sleeping man's handsome but careworn face she unwrapped the wound that Little John had sought to stanch, and, taking her lancet, she opened a vein in Robin's arm. Then, instead of binding the wonderful curative herbs round the wound, she hastily left the room and did not return.

All that night did Robin's life-blood flow, drop by drop, and not a soul came near to minister to him. In the morning, just as the sun peeped into the room, Robin woke, faint from the great loss of blood, and felt his end was near. Stretching out a hand, he grasped his horn and, leaning painfully upon his elbow, he blew a weak blast.

Faint as was the call, it reached Little John,

who was already on his way to see how his
comrade fared. Fearing some unknown evil,
the faithful man burst into the chamber where,
pale and dying, lay poor Robin.

"What treachery is this?" he called out
wildly, and, raising the weak body so that it
might find comfort in the immense strength
of the other, he exclaimed in tones of deepest
injury:

"My master, grant me yet a last boon—
that I drive these false nuns from their home
and burn this place to the ground!"

"Nay, friend!" whispered Robin painfully.
"Never — hath woman — been hurt — by me.
'Twere—too late—to begin," and the faintest
smile stole over his features for a moment and
then was gone.

Heartbroken, Little John nursed the sick
man, and watched him hour by hour as life
slowly ebbed away. At the close of the
sunny afternoon Robin started up from a deep
trance.

"John," said he firmly but weakly, "my
life—runs out—quickly. Carry me—to yon
window. Give me — my bow. String — an
arrow—on't."

Little John did so, and carried the dying
Robin to the window, which looked out upon

a fair meadow dotted here and there with fine old trees.

Supported by Little John, Robin wearily loosed the shaft, and the arrow sped slowly, and alighted under a spreading oak some fifty paces from the convent walls.

Seeing where the arrow fell, Robin whispered in a low voice:

"Bury me — where rests — my last — shaft. Lay—a green sod—'neath my head—and one—at my feet.   I shall—rest happy—now—I know —the winds of heaven—will stir—the leaves—of a greenwood—tree—above me."

Presently his eyes opened, and he smiled faintly at his friend.

"Good-bye—friend—Little John—Marian—is beckoning—and I—would go—to her."

Once more the glazed look came over his brave blue eyes, and the death sweat stood in great drops upon his forehead. Little John sobbed.   A gentle pressure of the hand and the noble spirit passed.

Robin Hood, truest and kindest of men, was no more.

Toward morning the bereaved man went out and digged a grave, even where the arrow had rested, and lovingly bore his master and laid him to rest.

Over the grave Little John set a stone, that generations yet unborn might know where the hero was laid to rest.

On the stone he carved in bold, deep letters:

HERE LIETH THE BODY OF ROBIN HOOD:
A BETTER MAN THERE NE'ER WAS ONE.
SUCH ARCHERS AS ROBIN AND HIS MEN
WILL ENGLAND NEVER SEE AGAIN.

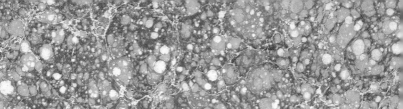